Restoring

the

Castle

Cyberworld Publishing

Cyberworld Publishing established 2009

www.cyberworldpublishing.com

This book is copyright Olivia Stowe © 2012
First published by Cyberworld Publishing in 2012
Cover design by S Bush © 2012
Cover photo: © Robbflynn | Dreamstime.com
E-book ISBN: 978-1-921879-24-1
Print ISBN: 978-1-921879-83-8

Cyberworld Publishing
16 Jindalee St
Toronto, NSW
Australia

Restoring

the

Castle

by

Olivia Stowe

Contents

Chapter One: Shattering the World

Khaki green was perhaps her least favorite color. So, why was her world swimming in it? "Swimming" was the word for the sensation, too. It seemed like she'd been swimming around in heavy water that was keeping her just below the surface despite all of her attempts to propel herself upward. The sensation felt like it had been going on forever.

Her eyes must be open. She wouldn't create a dream of various shades of khaki if her eyes were closed. The walls were a light khaki. The blanket was a darker khaki. The ceiling was . . . well it was sort of white. Those spongy tiles with the holes all over them. Like you would have found in a school or a hospital years ago.

A hospital. She felt it now. The pain and the heaviness were coming on in a slow wave. It seemed like her whole left side was weighted down by bandages. Those were white too. So, the whole world wasn't khaki after all. And the slender silver stand with the bottles and tubing hanging from it at her right side wasn't khaki either. Wondering where they were going, those tubes. But then thinking that was stupid. They were attached by needles to the veins in her hand and who knew where else? Coming increasingly close to the surface in her fight to get there through the pressure of whatever was holding her back. Hesitating, because there was increasing pain on the left side. Her whole left side. Her head too. A moment ago she hadn't realized it. But now she knew her head was pounding with pain. The left side of her head had bandaging around it too.

"Ally? Ally? Nurse! Nurse! Please, here. I think she's conscious."

"Mary?" Her eyes were focusing on the face of the woman hovering over hers. Well, her right eye was. There was some sort of bandage over the left eye. But who was Mary? Why had she said that when she'd seen the face?

"It's OK, Ally. I've called for the nurse. Someone will be here in a moment. Are you in pain? Can you hear me? Are you back with us?"

Of course. Mary. From the embassy. Mary Hendricks, the deputy chief of mission—the DCM. But why the concern? Mary had said no more than three sentences to Ally since the junior officer arrived at the embassy. Frigid, dismissive expressions. As if Ally wasn't even there, as if she was too peripheral to the business of the embassy to care about. What? Why? This wasn't the embassy—no room like she'd ever seen in the embassy.

8

"No, don't try to move yet, Ally. The nurses are coming. It's OK. You're going to be fine. The care here is great. You're in the military hospital in Landstuhl. The U.S. military hospital. In Germany. It's where they bring the American servicemen from Afghanistan and Iraq. They are great with bombing wounds. You're in exactly the right place."

Exactly the right place? For bomb victims?

The name she was trying to force out wasn't "Mary." It was a man's name. "Chad."

"Chad?" It was the first word she'd uttered in over a week.

Her eye was honing in on Mary Hendricks's face. She saw the intensification of the look of concern. The hardening of the edges around the mouth. Not noncommittally frigid today. She must really be worried about something.

"No excitement, Ally. You'll be fine. Here, the nurses are here now. Just take it slow."

The face of the deputy chief of mission of the U.S. Embassy in Amman, Jordan, disappeared from view to be replaced by those of two nurses, one female and one male—in khaki—bustling around her bed, checking this, adjusting that, and emitting clucking noises.

God how she hated the color khaki. But then that thought was replaced by something more urgent, more shocking. Remembering what Mary had said about her being in the right place. "Bomb," Mary Hendricks had said. Bomb wounds. Her left side.

"Chad," she said again, this time more as a moaned statement than a question.

And once again, none of the khaki-clad figures hovering about her gave her an answer.

* * * *

"It's a pity we have to rush back to Amman," Ally cried out to Chad over the noise of the Miata convertible's whining wheels. The road between the capital city of Jordan and the ancient city known to the Romans as Gerasa was a dusty, ill-maintained one. It had been known as Gerasa when it was one of the Decapolis cities—the ten cities across the Levant that served as the beads in the necklace of Rome's trading route into Asia proper. Now, as Jerash, it was sometimes incorrectly called the Pompeii of the Middle East because of how extensive and well preserved its ruins were. It was incorrectly called that because Pompeii was ruined by a volcanic eruption and Jerash by an earthquake in the eighth century.

Because of its ruins and because so much is still standing, Jerash exists as a major tourist destination in Jordan. And Alice, known by all as Ally, Templeton, the recently arrived cultural affairs officer at the U.S. embassy in Amman, Jordan, had just been given her first visit to the site by her newly minted fiancé, Chad Huntley, a political officer at the embassy. The trip was official, because Ally had a responsibility to master the cultural attractions of the country she was posted to. The two-night stay at the Hadrian's Gate Hotel, immediately across from that same-named victory arch gate marking the entrance into the ancient city ruins, was not official. But so smitten had the two become with each other, and so quickly, that few at the embassy were surprised they were running off together for intimate weekends. At least they had made their intentions official before leaving for this weekend jaunt when Chad had given Ally a ring at an embassy cocktail party.

"What's that you said?" Chad yelled back over the road noise. And then, when Ally couldn't make herself better heard, he said. "It's time for a stop anyway. There's a roadside restaurant up ahead. We'll stop for something to drink and a chance to shake the dust off."

"What did you try to tell me back on the road?" Chad asked when they were settled with bottles of beer under a vine-covered trellis on the roof veranda of the roadside restaurant.

"I said it's too bad we have to be back in Amman this afternoon. I haven't seen all of Jerash that I wanted to explore."

"There will be other visits to Jerash. Next you must see Petra in the south, though. That's the ultimate tourist destination in Jordan. But if I don't get you back for the Fulbright scholarship interviews this afternoon, the ambassador will have my hide—or the DCM will. Mary Hendricks cracks the whip harder than the ambassador does."

"She's certainly a dragon lady, isn't she? Wish she'd crack a smile now and again."

It was only when they were away from the embassy that they felt comfortable enough to talk of the second in command, the deputy chief of mission, like this.

"It's you who needs to be back for those interviews," Ally continued. "You've done them before; I haven't."

"But you have to chair the session, Ally. Besides Fulbright House needs your radiance. The interviewees will come in all nervous and trying to remember what their rich parents coached them to say about how indigent their family is."

"You're such a cynic," Ally said. But that's not what she was thinking when she was looking at him across the small table between them. She was thinking how lucky she was to land him. He was by far the best catch in the whole region of embassies—and she'd done a round of U.S. embassies in the Middle East in connection with her assignment in Amman. And the irony was that she hadn't been looking to catch anything.

He was suave without exuding conceit, and he had the strong, blond American athlete good looks that would justify conceit. She didn't know what he saw in her, but she hoped it would be enough to keep him. She'd been as far as the ring part of relationships before, but they had never worked out. More than one suitor had ended up saying that she was too much like her mother—too reserved and independent. An ice maiden. And her mother hadn't been a help there either. She'd been frosty with any man Ally had introduced her to.

She could see that any of the men who had been interested in her had been intimidated by Miranda, her mother. She could see it in her mother herself. But none of them knew the life her mother had had to face and the choices she had to make. Not that Ally knew it all herself; there were some discussions her mother refused to have.

Ally certainly wasn't being an ice maiden with Chad. She had never gone away for a weekend with a man before. She had sensed early on that this was the one—no one had both given her the space she needed and drawn her close when that was what she needed like Chad Huntley had done. He made her feel like a million dollars and like this posting to Amman was a fairy tale—a fairy tale dream she never wanted to wake up from.

She had resisted at first, thinking that both an attraction to and a connection with him were moving too fast. They had only known each other for a couple of months. But her best friend at the embassy, the economic officer had taken her aside one day and had said, "Why are you ignoring Chad? All of the other women here envy you—and hate you for seeming to be indifferent to his interest. You do know he's interested in you, don't you, Ally?"

"Not any more interested in me than I in he, Julie," Ally had responded. "But what will everyone think of me going head over heels for him in just a couple of months?"

"This is your first embassy assignment," Julie had said. "You just don't get the culture in the Foreign Service. We act decisively and move fast. The service is full of quick courtships and marriages."

"Oh," Ally had answered. It was only weeks later, though, after Chad and she were already a couple, that Julie added that the culture was just as quick to divorce. but by then Ally was completely lost to Chad.

"You'll be fine," Julie had said. "He's a catch in every way, and even if it doesn't work out, you'll have had fun that most of the other women here would die to enjoy."

"The Fulbright program breeds cynicism, Ally," Chad responded to the question that Ally, in her reverie had already forgotten she'd asked, although she felt guilty that she'd just been having cynical thoughts herself. "You'll see. On paper we are supposed to award scholarships to universities in the States on merit and need—and on the probability that the students will return home and make a big difference in the well-being of their country. But those applying for the scholarships play the system right under our eyes. They try to hide their family wealth in the paperwork and they roll up in Mercedes and BMWs for the interview. They don't try to hide any of it too hard, knowing that what we really want in a Fulbright scholar is someone from influence who is going to return to influence, plus having been Americanized and grateful to Uncle Sam. I can't fault them much. For a student in the Middle East to be competitive for a Fulbright scholarship, money-financed preparation is a given need. I don't think they realize that at home. There aren't too many poor people getting into national universities in the region and also able to do what it takes to stand out above the rich and privileged."

Chad looked up and smiled that radiant smile of his. "I've been prattling, haven't I?"

"Yes, but I love you when you are this intense about something. Your 'serious stuff' look is so cute. And I'm not really that turned off by the process. It's American money; I think we should get a good return on our investment. I think that we need our friends in positions of power worldwide and that this is a constructive way to achieve that—for everyone. I also rather think that they do understand the real dynamic at play back in Washington; they just find it politic to mouth the idealism of the Fulbright foundation documents."

"Ever the hardheaded, practical type, aren't you, Ally?"

"I think it makes us a good team," she answered.

"And I think you're right. But speaking of being practical—and I hate to return to it—but we really must make a decision on where the ceremony is to be. I hear you about your mother's delicate health. I'm perfectly willing to go to Virginia to marry. And I'm anxious to see the mother of the woman I'm going to marry."

Ally turned her head so that Chad couldn't see the expression on her face. Meeting her mother had been the worst aspect of all of this—and not one she was willing to face before she absolutely had to. She had exaggerated the "delicate health" excuse, unless her mother being generally contemptuous of men qualified.

"I continue to say we do it right here, among the mutual friends we have in the embassy, local, and expatriate community," she countered. "My mother's a recluse in the mountains. I've told you that. It isn't just that her condition is . . . unstable. I don't know how we could even scrape two witnesses together in Virginia. You've never been there, and I haven't been there in years. Not since I went into training for the Foreign Service."

"You make it sound all so mysterious," Chad said. "If I didn't know better, I'd think that you and your mother are estranged. Yet I know you call her occasionally—even from Jordan."

"Yes, we're close enough—from a distance. But she would hate all of the fuss; I know she would. I've talked to her. She wants us to marry here and get all of the pomp and circumstance over with and then visit her, just you and me. That's just the way she is. She was even that way when she was Recevich's secretary with the National Symphony. She was the calm in the storm with everything going on around her—efficiently getting what needed to be done but by being able to get away with pushing around all of the spoiled prima donnas who go along with the musical world."

"Ah, yes, I never can quite fathom that—the childhood you describe of traveling the world with your mother and symphony orchestras, knowing all those famous people and being homeschooled by your mother with the backdrop of all the great cities of the world as your schoolhouse."

"I never knew any other child was having a different kind of life, Chad. I didn't grow up around children."

"And it's why you seem to know everyone in the musical world—which makes you the ideal cultural affairs officer. All to the good."

"Yes, but I sometimes wonder what I missed by not having a normal childhood."

"And so you want to marry a child to see what it was like."

Ally turned and looked at him. He had such an "oh, gosh" lopsided grin on his face, that she had to laugh. "You've been anything but a child with me, you handsome devil. And that too is all to the good." She meant it, of course, but still, she had to admit that it was the carefree, childlike qualities in Chad that had attracted her to him in the first place. She fully realized she was a couple of years older than he was, but he had said that didn't make any difference to him—they even joked about it now. She had come to the diplomatic corps a few years later than most, as she had worked on Broadway for a few years after taking her masters degree.

They made good time back to Amman and each had time to go to their offices in the embassy to check their messages and the work piled on their respective desks before they met again in the embassy car pool to be driven over to Fulbright House. The base for the Fulbright program was in a villa in the quiet residential area of Shmeiseni. Much of the cultural and education program interaction with the Jordanians was conducted in this villa. All of the embassy's cultural and educational activities came under Ally's cultural affairs officer hat.

They kissed and cuddled in the backseat of the embassy car on the way over to the interviews and Chad whispered in Ally's ear what uses they could make of the plush interior of the tinted window sedan if they wanted to be naughty. Ally wanted to be naughty, but she knew they couldn't do so now and here. She knew that Chad was aware of that too. So, she contented herself with watching the exotic scenes of the crowded Arab street beyond the tinted windows of their official air conditioned sedan while fantasizing what she and Chad could be doing—some of which they *had* been doing the previous weekend in the Hadrian's Gate hotel room.

The local administrator of the semiannual Fulbright scholarship interviews ushered Ally to her seat at the head of the interview table, Chad slid into the seat to her left, and the other three official members of the program found seats around them.

The third interviewee who came in was a surprise to her. He was significantly more nervous than the others, had given a little cry of panic when he almost dropped his briefcase upon entering the room, and seemed distracted and singularly unprepared to talk about his engineering interests during the interview. He placed his briefcase down on the floor at his right side as he sat down at the table facing Ally, but he never opened and delved into the briefcase to respond to any of the questions the interviewers posed to him.

Ally didn't think of any significance there could be to that until more than two weeks later, but she distinctly remembered Chad murmuring as they were waiting for the next candidate to enter the room that the young man obviously wasn't up to the quality of prospective Fulbright scholars they were interviewing, which, he said, surprised him. According to the records on the student, the young man's family was prominent in Jordan and his academic and activities background were stellar. Ally hadn't been able to hear what Chad had said in sotto voce at first, and he'd leaned forward on the table and turned to her so that he could speak without any of the others hearing him.

Thus focused on each other, neither saw the student rise and hurry from the room.

Ally, having never been involved in Fulbright scholarship interviews before, turned into Chad to listen to what he was saying and to query him further on the obviously botched interview when she both heard and felt the explosion and her world evaporated into an intense white-hot light.

When the terrorist attack was pieced together later, it was discovered that the real interviewee had died in a suspicious traffic accident on the very morning of his scheduled interview. The young man who had shown up in his stead was later to appear, grinning ear to ear, on a film clip sent to Al Jazeera television by the never-before identified terrorist organization, the Muslim Spear, claiming responsibility for the bombing.

* * * *

"I have just a few questions, if you please, miss. Very little information was taken when you were flown in from Jordan. And it was an embassy, so the doctors got right to work without requiring some of the authorizations that servicemen need."

"That's fine. What do you need to know, sergeant? It is sergeant, isn't it?" Ally was peering at the woman soldier's name tag, trying to make out what it said. Her left eye was still covered, although she'd been told there was no permanent damage there— just that the blast had been so bright her cornea was bruised and would need to heal some more before it was exposed to light. In fact, she was told that plastic surgery had taken care of all of the bits of shrapnel that hit her face and leg, and that the only visible scaring she'd have would be on her left arm and torso—and that even that would heal so that the scaring would look more like a red rash than wounds from a bomb. Carefully applied cosmetics would pretty much take care of that if she needed to hide it.

What they didn't tell her was that she'd been saved from the worst of the blast because Chad had been sitting to the left of her and had taken its full force. She didn't have to be told that. She had figured that out herself from everyone's reticence to tell her about Chad other than that he was gone. The only mercy was that he must have been gone immediately.

"Well, we have the name Ally Hunt on the admittance form. The paramedics who came with you on the plane were the ones who provided the information—they say you were mumbling that. But the woman who came with them, the ambassador or someone, called you Ms. Templeton. And we can't get you to come up in the government databases. I think we should get that—"

"The woman who came with me is number two in the embassy. But Hunt? No I think they must have been mis—" But then she stopped speaking, in horror. She swallowed hard and in a small voice, "Perhaps the paramedics heard me trying to say Huntley. That was my fiancé's name. He was killed in the blast. We were supposed to be married soon, and . . ."

The sergeant put a hand on top of Ally's, letting her know she needn't go on. Ally looked over at the soldier and saw that her face was lowered so that Ally couldn't see her expression. She turned her hand and squeezed that of the soldier, grateful for the gesture and understanding that that woman was in uniform—that hated khaki—and probably couldn't show more emotion than that. She probably shouldn't be showing the emotion that she was unable to conceal.

Ally was so drained by emotion herself that she was just too tired to fall apart. She did manage to add, "I've probably been in the field for too short a time to have been listed in your databases. For your form, you'd better put Alice Templeton. Alice is my given name. I've just been going by the name Ally for so long that I rarely use the other name. Maybe you'll find me in the databases under Alice Templeton." She had purposely made her voice as steady and businesslike as possible—for the sergeant's benefit.

The sergeant wiped her eyes and nose as surreptitiously as she could with the sleeve of her khaki shirt and picked up her clipboard. "Thanks," she said—and both women knew what she was thankful for. "Mother's name?" she asked, back in her familiar groove.

"Miranda. Miranda Templeton."

"Father."

"You'll need to leave that blank."

"Excuse me?"

"I'm sorry. I have never been told who my father was. And no one was stepping up to the plate on that one, as far as I know. My mother always put her own name in the slot when we were forced to put something. And my mother was a big enough presence to qualify. So, if you must—"

"That's OK. I'll put 'unknown,'" the sergeant answered. "That's what the regs say to use."

"Fine. It doesn't bother me," Ally answered in the half-amused voice she had cultivated for just this situation. She had found that it cut off further discussion, which is exactly what she wanted it to do.

"Birthday?"

"Excuse me, sergeant. Could you step out for a few minutes. I wish to speak with the patient in private." An officer had come into the room and was standing behind the sergeant.

"Yes, of course, major," the sergeant said in a clipped, "yes, sir," manner. She rose quickly with her back ramrod straight and quickstepped out of the room.

The doctor, Major Jackson, a solidly built black man who had, the other doctors said, worked miracles on Ally's plastic surgery, had surprised both Ally and the sergeant by slipping into the room quietly, something he hadn't been prone to do before. His arrival was usually announced with trumpets. His demeanor today was serious and a little sad.

Ally was prepared for some bad news on her condition or recovery schedule.

Major Jackson sat down in the chair the sergeant had vacated, right at the edge of Ally's bed, and took her right hand in his.

"First," he said, "I want you to know that you can transfer back to the States as soon as you need to. We can arrange any follow-up that's needed. And you're coming along very well."

"That's good. But, what is this about? Am I about to be kicked out? Has State Department coverage reached the end here?"

"No, nothing like that. But . . . but, first—another first—I can tell you that she's fine. A bit of smoke inhalation, but she'll recover—probably before you are fully recovered yourself."

"What is it?" Why was it so hard for these people to step up to bad news? Didn't they know that in the face of Chad's death there was nothing that would knock Ally off her pins—not now, possibly not ever again? And she had been trained for this. Her mother had been the champion indoctrinator of staying tough and calm in the face of bad news.

Her mother.

"My god, You're telling me my mother has set herself on fire again?"

The major gave her a strange look. And then, after a short pause, he said, "Well, something like that. But she didn't burn herself—at least not badly. She was in a house fire."

"The castle? Well, yes, she burned most of the second story of that out years ago—and a good part of the downstairs more recently than that. That's hardly news."

"No, the house burned just a couple of days ago. She was pulled out of it by some sort of housekeeper, but she suffered smoke inhalation."

"Mrs. Aylor? Lois Aylor? She pulled my mother out? They were still in the castle? My mother was still living in the castle?"

"Yes, apparently so. But why do you call it 'the castle'? And you don't seem surprised."

"I'm not surprised, no. My mother's a chain smoker and nothing in the world has gotten in the way of that in her life. She goes to sleep smoking, and there's a fire. More than two decades ago she burned most of the second story off the castle completely, and seven years ago ruined most of the first floor too. I had no idea she was still living in it. And I called it the castle, because that's what it is. My mother lives in a castle—in the Blue Ridge Mountains of Virginia. Crazy, right? But that's my mother."

"So, what is it you want to do?" the major asked.

"I guess I need to go to Virginia at least long enough to see what's going on. As soon as you say I can go. State has given me a year's leave to decide what I want to do going forward. I can't go back to Amman. That's for sure."

Chapter Two: The Castle

She had just cleared the grape vines of the Mountain Castle winery and knew she was back on her mother's land for the first time in nearly seven years.

Ally stopped on the side of the narrow, winding, graveled road up into the mountains in a fold between the southern slope of Mount Marshall and a shorter mountain called The Peak, northwest of the small town of Washington. This quaint little hamlet on the verge between northern Virginia's hunt country and the Blue Ridge mountains wasn't the nation's capital Washington; it was a town also named Washington, but often called "Little Washington," with the distinction of being the first town to name itself after the first U.S. president.

It was only the small strip of land the road was on, though, that was her mother's land from the lane at the bottom of the mountain right up to the lower edge of the castle's front lawn. The Shenandoah National Park had slowly acquired all of the land around the small plateau the castle stood on so that it now encroached on all sides. The park had been after Miranda Templeton to donate or sell her land for decades, but, stubborn in nearly all things, Miranda had refused to even talk to them about it. Ally assumed that one day the government would just seize the land by right of eminent domain. She hoped her mother was gone before then, or there surely would be homicides involved.

She stepped out of the rental car and moved, with the aid of a cane, around to the hood. Initially her eyes went anywhere but up the slope to where, from here, the first full glimpse of the castle could be seen. Her own car, a BMW convertible, could have been gotten out of storage as soon as she'd arrived back in Washington, D.C. The State Department would have permitted that and then would have put it back in storage at its expense if she wanted if she went out on another foreign assignment. State had been great about everything. But Ally didn't want to do anything yet that moved toward a decision on her future having been made.

She wanted to take no steps toward permanence until she could work out in her mind where to go from here. Chad had been her decision on where to go. Thanks probably to her mother's strong attitudes on the topic, Chad had been the first man Ally had been intimate with—had even been let through her intellectual and emotional shell to any extent. When she had committed to him, she had jettisoned all that had been her before. Now that he was gone, she felt totally empty. She needed to reinvent herself again. She wasn't really sure how to even start doing that—or what direction to do it in. She was still in shock.

She'd been back a month, moving from Sibley Hospital, thanks to the arrangements that State had made, to a rehab facility, and then to a bedroom in a colleague's house in Arlington. She knew she couldn't stay there indefinitely, though. Only now, when she'd been given a clean bill of health, as long as she continued with a rehab regime for her leg at home, had she rented a car and driven into the northern Virginia countryside—not more than twenty-five miles from where she had been staying—to check up on her mother and the castle. She didn't know where she'd be staying tonight. She didn't even know where her mother was. She hadn't called her since the bombing. She hadn't been able to while she was in the hospital and being rehabilitated, and when she'd returned to the States she always seemed on the cusp of coming to see her mother face to face rather than calling. More significantly, her mother hadn't contacted her either. The doctor had said it was simple smoke inhalation that her mother had suffered from this latest fire. She should have recovered from that now. Surely State had contacted Miranda about Ally's condition. But she hadn't called. Such was the relationship between the two that this was exactly the sort of situation in which neither could think of what to say to the other.

Ally thought she knew the major reason her mother hadn't contacted her. It was the second serious fire. Ally had refused to come back to the castle after the second fire. She'd had no bones about being livid that her mother wouldn't give up her dangerous smoking habits. They had frequently met in New York City, while Ally was working on Broadway play sets there after graduate school and then later, in Washington, D.C., when Ally had taken and passed the Foreign Service exam, but the meetings were always away from the castle.

Although they'd made up since the first fire, Ally had been furious that her mother had burned out the part of the castle Ally had lived in—and had let her mother know in no uncertain terms how she felt. It had been the first time that Ally had spoken to her mother that way. The two women had been inseparable before that. Ally was thirty-six; she hadn't been a child for some time. Indeed, under her mother's wing and in her mother's swirling world of symphonies and international travel, Ally had never been a child. There had been no separation at all between them until Ally went off to study drama, and specifically set design, at Wellesley. And even after having taken her masters from Columbia following that, Miranda had been intimately involved in Ally's decisions to work on Broadway for a few years and then to go with the State Department to work in its cultural affairs department. It had only been Miranda's burning of the castle second time that had begun to open a chasm between them—which had only widened when Ally told Miranda about Chad. And now there had been yet another fire Miranda had caused.

Miranda hadn't reacted well to Ally having found a man to love. Not at all well. Over the past month, Ally had even

30

wondered whether the latest fire had been at least a subconscious signal by her mother on the impending change in Ally's marital status.

Steeling herself, Ally found the strength to look up the slope at the castle. From this distance it looked intact. The fires hadn't destroyed the stucco-covered stone façade. It was only by looking more closely that Ally could see the blank stares of the glassless windows, which, in several places, no longer opened onto a roof-covered interior. She had purposely stopped here to look at the castle, and to squint her eyes in doing so. She could only take the ruination of it in degrees.

They called it the castle, although it did have a name—Banffy. And it wasn't really a castle in dimensions. It had been constructed as a scaled-down replica of a real castle in Transylvania. The larger, grander—but not more impressive; most certainly not in location—Transylvanian version had begun construction in 1437 and was built for one of the most prominent and powerful families in Transylvania for many centuries, the Banffys, whose patriarchs regularly were appointed as governors of the region. It began life as a typical stronghold bastion, but as wars became more sophisticated and organized, it was turned into a Baroque palace in the mid eighteenth century. Extensive renovations were undertaken to expand it and modify it into the Gothic Revival style in the mid nineteenth century.

This was the point at which the Virginia version of Banffy was conceived and executed. One of the architects on the nineteenth-century renovation of the Transylvanian version, Stephen Monyer, immigrated to Virginia. Looking for someplace that would remind him of the topography of Transylvania, he settled on the mid slope of the 3,300-foot-high Mount Marshall at the northern end of the Blue Ridge Mountains. His Virginia version was faithful to the redone Gothic Revival style of the original in every way except for scale. It was a hidden gem, tucked away in the folds of the eastern slopes of the Blue Ridge, the heights of which had been taken over by the federal government in the 1920s to carve out a national park extending from northern Virginia down to the Smokies in Georgia. The string of mountaintops was crowned by both a top-of-the-world parkway, named the Skyline Drive in the northern section and the Blue Ridge Parkway in the south, and a section of the Appalachian hiking trail that went from the far north to the far south of the country's eastern coast.

Previous owners of the American version of the castle, all generational members of the Monyer families, had stubbornly rebuffed the government's attempts to add the Banffy acreage to the park until the last of the Monyers had died, when the federal government was no longer budgeting for such acquisitions. Now everyone had more or less forgotten there was a castle hidden on the southern slope of Mount Marshall. Miranda Templeton had only heard about the castle when she was visiting friends in the town of Washington at the foot of the mountain. It was a time when she was looking for a retreat, if not necessarily a castle, as well as a time when she had inherited money to indulge herself in a remembrance of the many years she had traveled with symphony orchestras in Europe. So, she bought Banffy castle and devoted years to restoring the gardens—and, incrementally burning out the interior of the castle in unintentional acts of forgetfulness and in having only slapdash repairs made that moved her into ever-smaller habitable areas of the building.

It had been the news reports of the first fire that had alerted the park officials to the unfinished business of land acquisition on the side of Mount Marshall. After a few years of unsuccessfully working on Miranda to donate or sell, though, they had given up their interest yet again.

The building had never really been able to claim full habitability even during the three years Ally had lived there with her mother before going off to Wellesley. After the first fire, they essentially lived in two rooms and a kitchen downstairs and two bedrooms, Miranda's study, and a bath upstairs. But the rooms they did live in were elegantly outfitted and maintained. Ally had been there long enough, however, to be smitten by the minor grandeur and unique beauty of the building; the gardens, that her mother lovingly restored and maintained; and the quiet, private mountain beauty of its location. She had always dreamed of restoring the castle interior fully one day. But her mother's smoking habit and her eccentric willingness to "make do" had made that day an ever-more-remote possibility.

Ally returned to the driver's seat and started the car on its steep, hairpin-curved drive up to Banffy. As she drove, she tried—unsuccessfully—not to look at the castle as its ruination became increasingly apparent. Thus it was that, as she drew closer, she saw the tail end of a red truck disappear on a track into the forest at the upslope side of the property. It was only a glimpse, but it arrested her attention because she knew that the track went nowhere—or at least had gone nowhere when she'd lived here. Trekkers on the Appalachian Trail sometimes found their way down this track from the summit of Mount Marshall to be flabbergasted at coming out into the formal gardens of a small castle ruins, but vehicles couldn't get far on it now. It was part of an old, disused fire trail that had become overgrown and impassable even for jeeps.

She brought the rental car to a stop short of a yellow caution tape that had been strung in front of the castle—probably after the most recent fire. She could have gone on, as the tape was down on the ground across the driveway, but she didn't, almost as if she welcomed the instruction not to come closer to the structure.

Her heart ached as she sat there and looked at what had become of Banffy. On this, the front façade, both stories of the building were just a shell. She laughed a low, ironic laugh when it occurred to her that her home now closely resembled the palace it was modeled on—more than it had for a very long time. The Transylvania Banffy Castle had been gutted in World War II and only now was starting to be restored. Wouldn't it be something, she thought, if the two were being restored at the same time?

As she got out of the car, having worked up the courage to go inside and see what, if anything still existed, she heard the crunch of tires on the gravel of the mountain driveway. Turning, she saw that it was a sheriff's car. So, she stood by the fender of her car and waited for the other vehicle to come to a stop near her. Out of the cruiser, taking his time getting his bulk out from behind the steering wheel, emerged a florid-faced, bullet-headed, middle-aged man who Ally reasoned must be the local sheriff. No one else on the sheriff's staff would have been permitted to let themselves go to pot like this and still keep their job. In this county, she knew, the sheriff was elected—and anyone was free to run for the job.

The man walked around to the passenger side of his cruiser, but still a good six yards from where Ally stood. He tipped his hat and said, "Good day, miss. I'm Sheriff Ed Shiflet. Is there something I can help you with? This here is restricted property, I'm afraid."

"It's OK, sheriff. I'm Ally Templeton, the owner's daughter—well, a co-owner of the property. I've just now returned to Virginia to see what has happened here."

"Miranda Templeton's daughter? I wasn't aware Ms. Templeton had any children. As I said, this is restricted property—and the building there ain't real safe. The folks down at the winery saw your car go by and called me. I've been up a couple of times on vandalism calls in the last couple of weeks."

"I really am Miranda Templeton's daughter and a co-owner of this property. If it's OK for me to go into my purse, I can show you my license."

Shiflet nodded his head slightly, but he watched Ally like a hawk, one hand on the butt of the gun he had in an unfastened holster at his side. Ally had the sensation that she had stumbled into the gunfight at the OK Corral, and she almost giggled at the thought of this sloven man, with his belly flopping over his belt, as a movie gunslinger.

Handing her license back, the sheriff simply said, "OK, then. As I said, I didn't realize that Ms. Templeton had any children."

"Mother isn't too open about her life."

"Don't I know it," the sheriff said. There was nothing in his tone that should have given offense, and he wasn't saying anything that wasn't the truth, but Ally's irritation welled up inside her and she felt herself going on the offensive. Which was a surprise to her. She didn't often feel the need to defend her mother. Her mother didn't often need help defending herself.

"I was just checking on the castle," she said, turning from Shiflet so he couldn't see her frown. "I've been overseas—with an embassy—and I heard about the fire but had no idea how extensive the damage was."

"If you ask me, what it needs is a couple of sticks of dynamite to bring down whatever hasn't collapsed on its own. It ain't safe and it ain't exactly in keeping with the countryside around here. Bet you could strike a deal with the government to sell it to them for park land. It's almost completely surrounded by the national park as it is."

Thinking back later, that was probably the very first inkling Ally had that she wouldn't be taking the building down—or selling or giving it to the park. Just from what the sheriff said and how he'd said it, she knew that she had come back to restore the castle—to make it better than her mother had ever done. She'd have to get someone else for the gardens, but she'd see to the house herself. Everyone would say she couldn't do it, but she was her mother's daughter. That would be just the challenge she'd need to get it done. She was good with construction and tools. That too very few would believe who just looked at her, who didn't know her. But she'd majored in set design, and not just in drawing them. She had learned how to build them, and she'd loved doing so. What she couldn't do herself, she could contract out.

All of this flashed through her mind in an instant. She had zoned out on what the sheriff was saying completely.

"I suggest you tell Ms. Templeton that—your mother. We can't have deputies coming up here on every suspicious call. We'll have to start sending bills on that. And it won't be long before I should be filing reports that will get the judge to order a

37

condemnation notice on the structure. It ain't safe. Some fool of a vandal is gonna get his neck broke in there, and the papers will be saying it's my department's fault. So you tell your mother—"

"I don't even know where my mother is, sheriff. I just got back in the country and I haven't heard anything from her since the fire. Do you have any idea where she is?"

"As far as I know, she's down at Lois Aylor's farm outside Washington. Lois is the one that pulled her out of the fire, and she's the one that's been watchin' over your mother for a year or more."

"Watching over my mother? I wasn't aware she needed watching over."

"You haven't talked to her for some time, have you?" There was a glint of victory in his eye, as if he still wasn't convinced that Ally was Miranda's daughter—that he wanted to catch her up in some misstep on that claim. But rather than either of them getting into that territory any further, he returned to his previous concern. "When you see her, you tell her that it's time for that eyesore to come down. Never has fit in around here, and I'm tired of all the happenings connected with it."

"The happenings connected with it?"

"I've had my eye on this place for years, yes I have. It's always been a worry in the back of my head. And don't think I haven't had my eye on that mother of yours too. There's been men disappearing up around here. And never be'in seen again or any reason found out."

"I don't know what you mean."

"Well, for starters you could ask Lois Aylor about whatever happened to that husband of hers—that Felix Aylor that your mother fought so hard with. But I don't really have time to jaw about here. I suggest you not try going in there, and you tell Ms. Templeton what I said, you hear—or get Ms. Aylor to at least try to get that through to her. And if you're a co-owner as you claim, I suggest you need to get something done before the judge loses his patience."

Ally said nothing; she just stood there looking at the sheriff with a deadpan expression on her face, but her mind racing trying to make out half of what he had been saying, as he wedged himself back under the wheel of his car, took off at gravel-screeching speed back down the hairpin curves, and disappeared between the stands of grape vines at the edge of the Templeton property.

After a minute of trying to control her anger and clear her mind, Ally turned and marched toward the bleak façade of the castle. No hick of an elected country sheriff was going to tell her she couldn't enter her own home.

* * * *

Passing through the front door was like entering a war zone. In the house as Ally had known it, you entered, through a one-story entrance hall, to a two-story grand foyer in the center of the main structure with a double curved staircase floating up to second-floor balconied walkways on all four sides. It had been built of stone, so the staircase was still there. But it just led up to open sky now where there had once been an ornate copper cage with stained-glass inserts. The downstairs rooms they had lived in were shotgunned to the back of the building behind double doors that were no longer there. First was a double parlor that was a scaled-down version of the ballroom in the original castle. The base of a circular tower led off at the front corner of the room. They had called this the music room; her mother's Petrof grand piano had been positioned in the center of the circular tower floor before she burned the sweet-sounding instrument to a crisp. Beyond that was a large, formal dining room. And then came the room Ally and her mother had virtually lived in, which was an enormous kitchen, large enough to include a living area off of it, centered around a fireplace with a Franklin stove insert. In the winter, this had heated that room, which was the only livable portion of the castle in cold weather.

Upstairs, in what was now open air, had been three rooms and a bath across the front façade of the castle. Miranda's study had been in the western corner, which included the second story of the conical-roofed tower; then her bedroom, over the entrance hall, which opened off the landing at the top of the grand staircase; the bathroom; and in the eastern corner, Ally's bedroom. All of these rooms were huge and it would have been impossible to heat them in the winter. The women slept on studio couches in their kitchen when it was cold. Ally hadn't known till she went to college that this wasn't the way many Americans lived.

All of these rooms were seven years gone, gone up in the smoke from one of Miranda's forgotten cigarettes.

After walking through the downstairs areas she had known and seeing that the walls were still there, but no ceiling or roof, Ally went to the other side of the grand foyer, on the east side, where there had once been a drawing room, now in no better or worse condition than the rooms she had once lived in. Beyond that had been a library and billiards room and then the entry into what originally was the servants' wing.

This was where Ally found her mother had been living since the second fire. There was the servants' kitchen and dining room combined, which was large enough for Ally's mother to have made into a cozy living area. This, miraculously, was in good condition still. Beyond that were a series of smaller rooms, originally servants' rooms on both the first and second floor. One of them, immediately off the kitchen-living area, was the base of a circular tower, a faithful replica of one of the original, and crudely made towers in the oldest section of the original castle. This tower had risen four stories, but her mother's latest fire had burned out all of the wood flooring up to the stone ceiling, above which was an open-air battlement. The tower area had made for a rather large bedroom for Miranda, and she'd made a bathroom out of a servant's room off that. This was the room that had sustained most of the damage in the most recent fire. Standing in the center of it next to a charred bedstead, Ally was able to look straight up four stories to an opening to the sky that had been the top of the original staircase.

It was a mess, but the more she looked around the more she decided that this would be the easiest place to start with a restoration. She also could see that the first impressions were the worst—that most of the walls were sound and that even some of the roofing was still in place. Most of the fire damage in her mother's quarters had been in the tower. The kitchen-living area was essentially livable if she could get electricity and water hooked backed up there, and, with a couple of weeks of work—and a subcontractor in to put the flooring above the tower bedroom again, Ally could see herself living here while she worked to get the rest of the castle restored.

She was seeing this as a project to more than occupy her time and attention—to dominate it and push out all the thoughts and griefs that were plaguing her about her lost life with Chad—and perhaps her Foreign Service career too. It wasn't clear yet whether her injuries would ever be healed enough for her to pass an overseas physical. She could always take a Stateside job with the Department or go on medical disability with a very comfortable annuity—since she had been injured on the job—added to a sizable nest egg her mother had built for her from the inheritances they had unexpectedly received from Ally's grandfather. But she couldn't see herself trapped in a limiting job in Washington, D.C., or just living totally off an annuity, plus the sizable family inheritance her mother had barely touched, and doing nothing.

She would restore the castle. It may take millions, but it was just money, and Ally, like her mother had always lived frugally. She had a year to work on this before she had to take a physical or make any commitment one way or the other to the State Department. She would restore the castle, not having any idea what to do with it afterward—she was sure she didn't want to live here—but she would undertake it as a project to keep her sane and productive.

Ally returned to her mother's latest kitchen-living area and moved her eyes around, picking out cherished bits and pieces of her shared life with her mother. If there had been vandals here, they hadn't found this section of the house yet. There was a lock on the door she had come in by. She'd have to find the key to that. It should be somewhere in this room. She'd lock the room off to discourage the vandals from finding it before she could return.

Running her hand along the mantle of the fireplace in the sitting area Ally didn't find the key, but she found so much else that she remembered. There were photographs of her, with her mother, in various stages of her life. Photographs of her mother with both the symphony conductor who had originally hired her, August Donáti, and the one she'd worked for the longest, Misha Recevich. Photographs of her mother with her best friend, a symphony cellist, Angela Harris. And then various mementos of

Miranda's own early life in Manhattan and the European tours they had both taken. At the far end of the mantel was the old, engraved silver cup Miranda had taken everywhere, but didn't seem to like—the one with the initials "A.D." on one side and the words "Forgotten Never" on the other—bestowed, Ally had always assumed by a grateful employer, the National Symphony conductor, Donáti. Ally remembered having asked about it and seeing her mother get angry and taking it from her, returning it to its place, and telling her that good little girls didn't ask impertinent questions. As a curious little girl, though, Ally had only become more interested in that silver cup.

She would have thought more about that at this point, but the cup rattled when she picked it up—and that's where she found the key to the door. After looking around a bit more and almost coming to tears at the memories flooding up at her from what her mother had saved to decorate the space, Ally departed the room and locked the door behind her. She felt exhausted, and she still had that first meeting with her mother ahead of her. The sheriff had said she'd probably find her mother at Lois's farm. That had been what Ally had assumed too—that her mother would either be there or at Angela Harris's house in Little Washington She decided she'd try Lois's first.

When she came back out of the front door, she immediately saw the red truck, pulled up in the entry circle. Leaning against the fender, looking self-confident, handsome, and rugged, was a man of about forty-five with a tanned, weather-

44

beaten face, laughing blue eyes, and a toothy smile. He was wearing weathered jeans, a plaid lumberjack's shirt, and scruffed cowboy boots. If he'd been chewing on a corn stalk and swinging a lasso and had introduced himself as Will Rogers, Ally wouldn't have been surprised. Although his clothes looked well worn, they didn't look cheap or dirty. And he looked completely at home.

"Howdy," he said. "I'll bet you're the daughter."

"The daughter?" Ally said. "You mean Miranda Templeton's daughter? Yes, I am, but I don't know how you would know that, Mr. . . . ."

"I'm Jake Monroe. Of Monroe Construction. I know you because your mother must have had five photographs of you on her mantelpiece. And very proud of you, she was. She mentioned you constantly."

"I'm sorry, Mr. Monroe. I'm afraid I'm at a disadvantage." The man had no idea how great her disadvantage was, Ally thought. Who was he to have been in her mother's hidden suite in the castle and in contact with her mother? Her mother was an inveterate man hater. And this man exuded confidence and sensuality. She felt his eyes undressing her even as they stood there. He was both frightening and compelling. And she had no idea why. Had her mother succumbed to the charms of a man so late in life? Some sort of reaction to Ally going off to college and not returning perhaps? Or in revenge for those few men Ally had told her about seeing before she realized that such discussion with her mother was unwelcome?

45

"I was a contractor for your mother. Or my company was. Me and my brother, Craig. Well, my half brother. We got your mother set up in the first floor there, west side back, after her fire upstairs a few years back. I thought we did a good job, but she didn't like it and had us redo rooms over in the back east wing. And damned if she didn't sack us half through because we didn't agree on something and bring someone else in to finish redoing those rooms. A stubborn woman that. You wouldn't take after her on that, would you?"

Ally laughed. "I guess you did know my mother then. And, as a matter of fact, I am planning to restore the place. Not just a few rooms like mother always did. I want to redo the whole castle, bring it back to what it was in the beginning."

"That's quite a job. I wouldn't mind bidding on that," Jake said.

"I don't need a contractor. But I'll need subcontractors. I'll do the contracting myself. And I'll need construction workers. I only have a year to get it completed."

Monroe gave a little whistle. "A year to get this restored. That's biting off quite a bit. An architect are you?"

"No. A set designer." When he gave her a quizzical look, she clarified. "A stage set designer. The principles are pretty much the same, though. And I know my way around construction. And . . ."

"And, yup, I can see that you're your mother's daughter."

They both laughed at that. And Ally felt the tension going out of her body. She liked this easygoing guy. And although he was several years older than she was, she found him easy on the eyes too. She surprised herself. This was the first time since Chad that she'd looked at any man with that sort of interest. But she was finding it easy to show interest in this Jake Monroe. He seemed so authentic. The sheriff had seemed stereotypical—and much the chauvinist. Ally thought that Jake was probably just as chauvinistic and controlling, but in a much more enticing way.

Or maybe it was just that she was tired. Tired of being tired and on edge. And of grieving all of the time.

"Well, I'd like the chance to bid on subcontracting jobs then, if it's OK with you. I've grown quite fond of this pile of rocks."

Ally smiled. The sheriff had wanted her to knock it down. Here stood Jake Monroe, voicing his willingness—and interest—in standing it up again. He couldn't have come at a better time or said anything that she more wanted to hear.

"I'd be happy to take your bids when I figure out what I want done, and in what order."

"Well then, here's my card. Call me as soon as you are ready with plans and need bids." He pulled himself off the fender of the car in a graceful move and moved to her, hand extended with a business card. Ally involuntarily sucked her breath in as he came close. He smelled pine scent clean, and she felt a tingling sensation at the nearness of him, half expecting him to envelop her in his arms. Half wanting him too.

But he didn't. He just smiled, tipped his hat, and moved to the driver's door of his truck.

"I saw you drive your truck up into the woods when I was driving up," she blurted out. It was a cross between a statement and an accusation, not a question. And it surprised the hell out of her that she'd posed it. If it had either surprised or irritated Jake, though, he didn't show it.

He just turned back to her, gave her a mischievous look, and said, "I saw your car approaching, but, more important, I saw the sheriff coming up the drive as well. Now, I didn't have any concern about your car, but I like to keep a county between me and that sheriff. We aren't exactly bosom buddies."

Giving her a close look as if daring her to pursue the question, his face went all smiley when she didn't. He tipped his hat again, climbed in the truck, and slowly pulled out of the circle, crossing the downed yellow tape and inching past her rental car.

Ally stood there, watching him go and chastising herself for falling under his charm. But charm he had aplenty. And he appeared not to like the sheriff any more than she, on first contact, had done. Not just a smooth, handsome devil, but perhaps a naughty boy as well. Ally knew she should be ashamed of herself for being attracted. But her first thought had been that her mother would be livid and go into one of her rants about the evil of men—and especially of men like Jake Monroe. Somehow, that didn't attract Ally to Jake Monroe any less.

Chapter Three: Miranda

Ally drove down the mountain and found Lois Aylor's farm on the road just before entering the northern outskirts of the village of Washington. It was only with some difficulty that she found it, because she hadn't been there in years. There was a new Mercedes sedan parked by the door to the farmhouse that couldn't be either Lois's or her mother's, so she was hesitant to go in. But as she was sitting there wondering what she should do, she recognized her mother's old friend Angela Harris coming out of the door of the farmhouse—and waving when she saw and recognized Ally.

Angela Harris had, for as long as Ally had been aware, been Miranda's only close friend. She was a cellist with the National Symphony for most of the years Miranda had been the conductor's private secretary, and her husband, Dennis, had been first chair in the violin section. Ally didn't remember Dennis being around much—or being too attentive when he was there—but

Angela and Miranda had been almost inseparable. The Harrises had moved to the little town of Washington first, buying an elegant, perfectly symmetrical eighteenth-century Georgian brick home named Shadow Hill on the western outskirts of the small town. It had been Angela who found the decaying Banffy during a walk up into the mountains and had decided it would be the perfect retreat for Miranda.

Waving back and exiting her rental car, Ally was sure now that her mother indeed was staying with Lois. There was a slight moment of wondering why Miranda wasn't staying with Angela, but then it occurred to her that Dennis possibly was the answer. As far back as Ally could remember, she'd never seen her mother and Dennis in the same room together. Ally had put it down to her mother's response to every man other than the two great conductors she had devoted her life to—and the lack of any relationship was probably no better symbolized than that Angela had been Ally's godmother, but there quite pointedly had been no godfather designated. And if there had been, Ally was sure it wouldn't have been Dennis Harris. He had also been stiff with her to the point of seeming to shrink away from her when they were in proximity. He was always going off to practice his violin in his remote study in the house—or saying that he had to.

"Ally! You're home!"

"Hi, Angela, it's good to see you. You're looking great." And indeed she was. She'd always been a beautiful woman, groomed to the nines, and time hadn't changed that. She was as smart looking in gray hair and a gray silk suit and fuchsia-colored silk blouse as she had been in her black satin symphony dress.

"And you . . . you're looking . . ." Angela stopped as she took notice of the cane and the limp as Ally moved toward her. She obviously had temporarily forgotten about what had happened to Ally, but her face flooded with genuine concern when she remembered, and, loving her, Ally brushed by the embarrassment and came in for a hug.

"You've just been to see mother?"

"Yes."

"And how was she?"

"Don't expect too much, Ally. You've been gone for several years. And your mother . . ."

"Is my mother," Ally completed for her. Ally laughed and Angela smiled, but there was something in the strain evident in her face that surprised Ally.

"Just remember that your mother loves you very much, Ally. You are the world to her and there was no one else she talked about those years you were in college, working on Broadway, and starting off at the State Department. But the passage of time is something we can do nothing about."

"You seem to be able to. You haven't aged a day since I last saw you." The conversation had been getting uncomfortable for Ally—Angela seemed to known Miranda so much differently than Ally did. She saw nothing to be done but to try to lighten the conversation again. Was there something Angela couldn't bring herself to say? Did Miranda begrudge Ally going off to begin her own life? She had almost literally pushed Ally off on her own, but had Ally misinterpreted that as bravado she secretly wanted Ally to reject? Was it because of Chad? Or perhaps Miranda hadn't fared as well in the fire as others were saying.

"Liar," Angela responded with at least half a smile. "We all age. Some just have to spend twice as long at the beauty parlor in old age as they did when they were younger. Go on into her; don't let me keep you. But I must ask and I should have asked before now—do you have someplace to stay? I don't think that Lois has . . ."

"I've been to the castle. I think it won't be too difficult to fix up the rooms mother was staying in. I can stay there while I . . . Angela, I've decided I want to restore the castle. Not to what it was when mother had it. Back to the way it was originally."

"Why ever for?" Angela asked, her voice full of surprise.

"Not to keep it and live in it, but as a project. I need to get beyond the recent past. I need a project—a big one."

"I see. So you won't be with us permanently?"

"Who knows. I have a year to decide that. But I need something to work on right now."

"I can see that you're serious about this. And, if so, more power to you. I'd love to see that old place restored. But you can't start living up there immediately. Come stay with me if you don't have other plans. I'd love to have someone in the house again."

"Dennis?"

"Is living in Prague. Permanently now. And we are both the happier for it. We both thought that forty years was enough of an attempt to make a bad idea work out. You know he came from Prague originally."

"He came from Prague? With the name Harris? I always thought that was a British accent he was practicing."

"No, not British," Angela said with a light laugh. "He took an American name because the symphony was saying it had too many Europeans in it when they were holding auditions. He took the name off the door of the office across the hall where they were holding auditions when he overheard that remark. It's perhaps the only amusing thing that Dennis ever did. Perhaps if there had been more humor in his life. . . . He of course had his name changed legally later—after his audition was successful. But enough of that. If you haven't promised to stay with anyone else until you have accommodations fixed up at the castle, then you simply must stay with me."

Ally wasn't about to let the invitation go by twice without grabbing at it. She had hoped that she could stay a bit at Shadow Hill. The only thing that had kept her from asking was the presence of the glowering Dennis—which no longer was an issue.

"Yes, certainly. And thanks. I haven't any plans, actually. I'm very much in a 'winging it' phase these days. Just taking each day as it comes."

"Remember that when you go in to see your mother," Angela said, her face returning to its serious mode. "We're all taking it as each day comes now. Your mother no less than others."

Promising to be along to Angela's house in no more than an hour, Ally stood and waved the Mercedes off down the road— wondering what Angela was trying to convey to her about her mother.

It didn't take long to find out.

* * * *

Lois met her at the door.

"I'm so pleased you've come, Ms. Templeton."

"Ally, please, Mrs. Aylor."

"Only if it's Lois to you. Any time you could come is a good time, of course, but I'm afraid this isn't one of your mother's better days."

"Not one of her better days? Has my mother not recovered from the fire."

"Oh, yes, indeed she has. She's no worse than before the fire."

"No worse? What do you mean?"

"Oh, my, has no one told you about your mother?"

"I haven't heard from or about my mother since before the fire. Mrs. Harris hinted at something wrong just now, as we were standing by our cars, but that was the first inkling I've had that something is amiss with Mother."

"Oh, of course. I should have realized. You were always good to call on such a regular schedule. And she worked so hard to be ready for those calls the last few months. You know your mother—a will of steel. If she had to appear normal, she jolly would force herself to appear normal—at least until the last couple of months."

"What are you saying, Lois?"

"Your mother has dementia, the poor dear. It still comes and goes, but the doctors say it will only get worse. I'm afraid she is drifting away from us, the poor darling."

"Where is she?" Ally couldn't think of anything else to say. If she hadn't been built of the same strong steel that her mother was, she might have just sunk to the floor here in Lois's front hallway. This had to be the worst year of her life.

She put on a brave smile as Lois led her out to the enclosed sun porch, where Miranda Templeton sat at a table—dressed to the nines just as her friend Angela had been—but concentrating closely on sorting buttons from a big box packed with the multicolor circles.

Ally wanted to cry. Her mother had never given two figs for sewing. She was probably the least domesticated woman Ally had ever met. But she fought the tears away.

Seeing Ally's distress, Lois turned her face to her and murmured, "It helps keep her hands busy. She hasn't given up smoking willingly. I just won't allow them in the house. I'd rather it not be my house that's burnt to a crisp. So I try to keep her hands busy."

"Oh, yes, of course," Ally whispered back. She went over and sat down beside her mother and started sorting buttons herself.

"And who is this sweet woman you've brought to help me, Lois?" Miranda said, looking up with an angelic smile such as Ally had never before seen on her mother's face, but with eyes that were blank.

"It's your daughter, Ally. Come home to you," Lois answered. "Isn't that nice?"

"That's nice," Miranda parroted.

Ally proceeded to talk for a half hour, telling her mother about all of the good things that had happened to her since they last were together—and none of the bad.

Miranda said little other than nodding occasionally and making sounds of agreement and pleasure. At the end of the visit, when Ally rose to leave, saying she would come back to visit the next day and was staying with Angela Harris for a while, Miranda looked up, gave her a radiant smile, and said, "You sound like you have such a wonderful time living abroad, dear. You know I used to travel extensively in Europe with my daughter, Ally. You must meet her someday. You could share such wonderful stories about your travels."

Ally couldn't leave the room fast enough.

In the hallway, Lois took her arm and said, "Please don't take that as how it always is. When you come tomorrow, she is likely to be sharp as a tack and you can start all over as if today didn't exist."

"I guess that's what Angela meant by taking up what I'd said to her and applying it to mother—taking life one day at a time."

"No doubt. Mrs. Harris remains the one person your mother knows each time she visits. There are days that she reintroduces herself to me even."

"It's so good of you to be taking care of my mother like this."

"We thought it was for the best, Mrs. Harris and I—and the judge."

"The judge?" Ally said that a bit louder than she had intended. It came as a shock to her.

"Yes, well, after the fire and all. And you not being here and being in the hospital and in a bad way yourself for so long . . . and not having anyone else to take family responsibility. The court said something had to be done. And me being her housekeeper already and a nurse and having experience in what this is. And I can certainly use the money . . . there's plenty in her estate, they say. But with you back and all . . ."

"No, please, Lois. Let's leave it this way for now, as long as you are willing. I wouldn't know where to begin, and there's so much to do with the castle and all. And I have my own therapy needs."

"Don't say a word, dear. I love having her here—as long as we can keep her away from cigarettes and matches, of course. I've been with her for some time, and I rather enjoy growing old with her—what with my Felix gone and maybe not coming back."

"Yes, your Felix. Gone?"

"Yes, just up and left me one night. I've all along thought it was the drink. And he was a mean one when he drank—and that it set his mind on other women and what he thought would be a better life than with me. But you should have seen how your mother would sort him out when he got that way—with the drinking . . . and looking to other women." She paused and looked Ally in the face. "But listen to me. Gossiping about like this. And it's all water under the bridge it is. You said you are going up to Mrs. Harris's to stay a bit? Maybe I could call there in the morning and let you know how Ms. Templeton is. It changes from day to day, and there's little use of you coming unless it's a good day. Mrs. Harris is another matter. It's always a good day for whatever time Mrs. Harris can come. But there's no need to distress your mother if—"

"Yes, I understand—and completely agree, Lois. Again, you are an angel to be taking care of her."

They were shuffling toward the front door and had reached it when Lois Aylor gave a little exclamation and said, "Oh mercy me, I almost forgot. Can you hang on for a second? I have something to give you. It's been burning a hole in my memory banks, it has."

When she returned, she was holding an old stereo vinyl record in a faded cover. "Here. Your mother asked me to hold this and give to you after she . . . after she was gone. But I know these cases. Chances are good I'll go before she does. She might outlive us all as strong willed as she is underneath it all. And it's burning a hole in my remembrances. I think and worry about it nearly every day. I've been so afraid I would mislay it or forget ever to give it to you or something. Truth of the matter is that she's mostly gone now anyway, the poor woman. So, if you don't mind, I'll give it over now. You can do what you want with it."

"A record? How strange," Ally said, turning the jacket from one side to the other, trying to focus on it. "It's a 33 1/3 recording of violin concertos. How odd. I don't remember my mother being particularly taken with the violin. She seemed to prefer the cello, like Angela used to play. They don't seem to be notable works. The only one here that I think I've even heard of is this Edward Elgar piece. The 'Violin Concerto in B Minor, Opus 61.' Performed by the National Symphony, though, under August Donáti. Recorded in 1976. How extraordinary. And you say that mother explicitly said she wanted it to go to me?"

"Yes, and I'm sure it was very important to her, it was."

"Did she say so?" Ally was still quite perplexed. This was a conundrum she really didn't need on top of the shocks she'd had this afternoon already.

"Not in words, no, but in action."

"In action?"

"It was lucky that I was coming to do some housework for her the day of that fire. If I hadn't come in in time, who knows what would have happened to the poor dear. The flames had already gotten to the curtains. But did she panic when I woke her? No, not her. She walked straight over to a bureau and fished out this record, clutched it to her chest, and suggested that perhaps we should leave. That there record was the only thing she'd tried to save. With us not knowing that the fire would be contained so quickly. It was mostly the smoke that was a danger. She clutched that record to her all the time the medics were giving her oxygen in the back of the ambulance. And it was during the ride down the mountain and to a hospital that she handed it over to me and, with the first breath she could manage to take without choking, told me to hold it for you."

"How extraordinary," Ally said, as she stood on the front stoop of Lois's house. And as exhausted and overwrought as she was—and not being able to reveal that to Lois Aylor—that's the only phrase she could think of during the short drive through the north end of the village of Washington, turning at the corner where the five-star boutique Inn at Little Washington stood, and then heading out the west end of the town to Shadow Hill, Angela Harris's Georgian manor house. How extraordinary, she kept turning over in her mind. How extraordinary indeed.

* * * *

"What do you have there?" Angela asked when she answered her door and let Ally in.

"I'm not sure," Ally answered. She was somewhat in a daze still and had climbed the front steps clutching the record jacket and forgetting that she had luggage in the trunk of the car. "It's a record. Lois gave it to me. She said that mother said she wanted me to have it—that it was the one thing my mother tried to save from the fire."

"Here, let me see it."

Ally could see Angela blanch after she had closely examined the record.

"What is it, Angela? Do you know the significance of mother wanting me to have it?"

Angela seemed unable to decide how to respond because her face took on a set aspect—a little smile that Ally didn't really believe and was surprised to see. Angela didn't normally give false smiles, and wasn't all that good at it.

"No, I have no idea—other than the memory value of it. She was working for the National Symphony at the time and 1976 was the year of your birth. I would suppose she just saw some significance in those two facts coming together."

"Were you with the symphony then? And was Dennis? Do you think you are playing on this recording."

"That's possible, of course. I don't remember, though. It was so long ago and there were so many recording sessions. But enough of that. Let's get you and your luggage in the house. It looks like it might rain. You may remember Virginia and its late spring afternoon thunderstorms. They come over the mountains fast and with little notice, bang about something terrible, and are gone again almost as quickly as they arrive. But for all of the noise, they can be destructive. I don't know how many trees we've lost in the village this spring alone—some of them were there when George Washington was still astride a horse, I wouldn't be surprised. I'll take you up to your room. You look like you could use a nap. And after today's events I'm sure you can. Supper will be at eight and I don't expect you downstairs a moment before that unless you want to come down for a drink first."

And I think you know something you're not telling, Ally thought, as the two women descended the front stairs to the circular drive for the luggage. But Angela was right; she was entirely too tired to pursue the issue further—at least now.

After she'd gotten upstairs, unpacked, and showered, though, she found she wasn't sleepy. She knew this would last for only a few moments, that she was actually on the verge of collapse and it had only been the shower that had momentarily revived her. She sat down on the bed and took another, close, look at the record jacket. Angela must not have been reading it too well, she thought. It was right there on the jacket under the credits. A violin solo featured in the Elgar concerto she was familiar with. And there, right in the credits, it showed that Dennis Harris had been the violin soloist.

I'll have to remember to tell Angela that Dennis—and therefore probably Angela too—had played on the recording, she was thinking as she drifted off to sleep—to dream what was becoming a recurring nightmare. In her dream Chad was leaning toward her, smiling, his lips coming closer. And then, puff, he was gone.

She appeared for dinner a few minutes early and, as Angela and the cook were making last-minute preparations in the kitchen, Ally walked around the large, formal dining room, peering into the various glass-fronted cases on the side walls that contained decades of mementos and trophies the Harrises had collected in their successful symphony days.

As she was walking down the line of cases, she stopped and did a double take. Her attention was arrested by a set of silver cups. It was the second time today she'd seen a silver cup with such a unique shape. There were seven of them, and they were a match to the one on her mother's mantelpiece at the castle. They were all obviously very old, just as her mother's was, and they were all turned so that the side showing the initials "A.D." was facing the observer. Ally had an urge to open the case and see if they had the same inscription on the other side that her mother's did: "Forgotten Never." But the case was locked. Also at that moment Angela and the cook were coming into the dining room from the kitchen, carrying more plates and bowls of food than two women watching their figures could possibly do justice to. Ally tucked into her brain a question for Angela on what the story was behind those silver cups—and how their mate had come to be one of her own mother's most cherished possessions.

But during dinner she asked another question first, and the answer to that sent her brain spinning so fast that she forgot the silver cup question altogether.

"A curse of the castle?" Angela inclined her head and asked. She seemed definitely intrigued by the question.

"Yes, the county sheriff was up at the castle this afternoon when I was there. He was complaining about the number of times he'd had to come up to the castle. And he said something about men disappearing up there. Do you have any idea what he meant by that?"

Angela took her time responding. She patted at her mouth with her napkin and then brushed the napkin out flat on her lap while choosing her words.

"I doubt that he means disappearances at the castle itself. But there have been cases over the last several years—most of them since you went off to college—of men with some link to the castle disappearing. And I guess your mother's reputation for not thinking much of men somehow has gotten mixed into that by the gossips. I certainly won't repeat all of the wild speculation some in the village have made of that. But, yes, there have been disappearances. All probably explainable."

"How many?"

"Three."

"That many? Who? And what connection did they have to Banffy?"

"Well, there's Lois Aylor's husband, Felix. But it's likely he just decided to take a hike up to the Appalachian Trail during one of his drunken spells and fell into a remote ravine."

"And the others?"

"There was a peculiar mountain man who lived up in one of the hollows. When they were creating the Shenandoah National Park across the crest of the Blue Ridge they displaced quite a few mountain families who didn't want to go. There's always been talk that some of them didn't go—that they just hunkered down in remote areas of the mountains and never have been found. There was a man doing handyman work around the village and area farms who was rumored to be one such mountain man. And he got a fixation on your mother. But he hasn't been around in years."

"Ah, yes, I vaguely remember such a man from when I lived here," Ally said. "He kept appearing on the lawn and just staring at Mother whenever she went out, and then he'd go away when she gave him a tongue lashing. But he'd come back after a time. And the third disappearance?"

"She had a couple of brothers, the Monroes, contracting for her in one of her occasional reconfigurations inside the castle. One of them disappeared while they were working on the castle. And apparently quite a bit of cash from the brothers' company also disappeared at the time. Of course most just assume he ran off with the cash."

"Would that be Jake Monroe's brother?"

"Yes. It was Craig Monroe. But what do you know about Jake? Did your mother tell you about her troubles with the Monroes?"

"No. Not a word. It seems that mother didn't tell me a lot of things going on in her life. No, Jake Monroe was up at the castle today. He's interested in subcontracting some of the work I need done. Is he not reliable? You mentioned that my mother had trouble with them."

"Your mother has trouble with anyone doing projects for her, I think we have to acknowledge. No one did work to her satisfaction. As far as I know Jake Monroe is reliable. He has a good reputation around here for the quality of his work and the fairness of his prices. It was really Craig Monroe who your mother was on the outs with. She thought he wasn't working all of the time she was paying him for. The brothers didn't get along too well with each other either, if I remember correctly."

"And why is it that mother and the castle are connected to these disappearance stories?"

"Unfortunately, your mother had a furious row with each one of the men right before they disappeared. The locals are good at connecting dots that aren't there, of course."

"Oh."

"And since you'll probably hear about it around the village if you have many dealings here, I might as well tell you something else." Angela put her cutlery down beside her plate and rearranged it and her glass and wine goblets to be "just so" straight before she continued.

"You probably need to know that there's some talk about Dennis too."

"What do you mean?"

"Dennis is gone too. And your mother and he had a knock-down-drag-out fight right before he left. Of course I tell anyone who will listen exactly where he is and that he's gone because of me, not your mother—and that I'm in frequent contact with him. But they don't really repeat the story in my presence, so there's not that much opportunity to set the record straight on that. And I'm not sure anyone from around here would put much credence in a defense I put up for your mother anyway."

Double oh, Ally thought. And she spent the rest of the meal mulling all of that over and forgot to say anything at all about the record jacket or the silver cups.

Chapter Four: Beginning

Ally woke up with the words on her lips. She realized she had actually mouthed them aloud. It had been some time—long before the bombing, even before she and Chad had gotten serious, since she had had the dream that had her saying the sentence over and over again. It was only now that she realized it had been that long.

"Who's my father?"

It had been the special phrase that she'd held close to her and had brought out to see the light of day only when she was mad at her mother—when she wanted to see her mother's mood darken. When she had the feeling that her relationship with her mother was too out of balance and she wasn't being given the proper consideration. And her mother would always stop dead in her tracks, whatever she was doing. She'd pull herself up and say, "You don't really want to know. Making one up would be so much better than the reality. Albert Einstein can be your father if that will make you feel smarter."

Once when her mother had really been in a rage over botched hotel arrangements when the symphony was playing in Vienna, Ally heard Miranda swear about some hotel functionary and saying, "Those East Europeans are all alike."

Ally had asked "alike like who?" and Miranda had said, "Like your father."

Miranda had immediately realized what she had said and had instantly calmed down and left the room, returning a short time later after she had taken charge and brought order out of chaos on the hotel arrangements pretending that she'd said nothing untoward before she left. But when Ally started to return to her question, dazed that her mother had revealed this much, Miranda severely shushed her and moved the discussion and the action to something else. The first chance Ally got, though, she'd sought out maps and books that would tell her where Eastern Europe was. It turned out to be a much bigger place than would readily reveal who her father was.

Fathers had always been a taboo topic between Miranda and Ally—and Ally only brought the subject up when she wanted to irritate her mother. It wasn't until Ally's teens, though, that she really considered the topic in relationship to her own father. A father was never mentioned as a family role, and Ally lived such an isolated life from other children and from family situations that it just didn't occur to her much that families traditionally came with a set of parents.

She was very much aware that Miranda hadn't had a father of her own but that she'd been raised in the large townhouse of her mother's Manhattan robber baron father among an extended family existing almost entirely of women except for Miranda's grandfather, a stern, foreboding figure who left little doubt that Miranda and her mother were under his roof at his sufferance. When Ally was very young, Miranda would tell her stories about her mean great-grandfather that would curl Ally's toes.

Miranda had been home schooled, so Ally was as well. When she'd come of age, Miranda had been shipped off to Wellesley, so naturally Ally had been too. But Miranda had studied musical composition and theory and Ally had rebelled to the extent that she took up theater arts—primarily stage design and construction. Miranda never got to finish college, though. Early in her senior year, her grandfather died and she and her mother were shipped off to less-wealthy, dry-as-toast maternal relatives in Minnesota. Miranda spoke of them not at all, and they were bland enough to slip off Ally's radar of family tree interest early in life. It was only years later, after a lengthy internal fight in the family that no one bothered to tell Miranda or her mother about that they found that Ally's great-grandfather had inexplicably left the two of them millions in trust funds.

Long before this came into light, though, Miranda had to have a job to hold up her mother's and her end in the household, her mother never having been trained for anything outside of the house, and in 1964 she managed to land a temporary assistant job with the forty-eight-year old conductor of the Minneapolis Symphony, August Donáti, a Hungarian-born conductor and composer. The two immediately hit it off and Miranda proved to be the perfect personal assistant and quickly received the job permanently. Donáti was on the move shortly thereafter, going first, to London to conduct the BBC Symphony, and then to Sweden to conduct the Stockholm Symphony and subsequently, in 1970, to Washington, D.C., and the National Symphony.

Miranda traveled the world with him, devoting her every waking moment to handling his personal affairs, seeing even more of him, some said, than did his concert pianist wife, Erica. Donáti was at the National Symphony until the late 1970s and then moved on to the Detroit Symphony. By that time, though, Miranda had somehow acquired a baby daughter of her own, born in 1976, and, even more surprising, didn't go with Donáti to Detroit. What she told people if they asked—and they certainly had to be either brave or stupid to dare to ask—why she hadn't gone to Detroit was that she'd had quite enough cold weather, thank you very much, when she'd lived in Minneapolis and Stockholm. Knowing how icy she could be even without the weather, people were content to accept this explanation.

She stayed in Washington, D.C., and became the rock for the new conductor of the National Symphony, the Russian-born cellist, Misha Recevich. Sometime in these years in Washington, she had become close friends with Angela and Dennis Harris.

Some said, rather cattily, that Miranda was a man hater even in those days and that her bitterness had interfered with her close working relationship with the conductor, a relationship that had also strained Donáti's marriage. All of this, of course, is inevitable among high strung, intensely professional musicians, Angela Harris had taken Miranda under her wing. She then became such a substitute intimate friend that, whereas such spats normally would be patched up and Miranda and Erica should have become close again, Angela now was too fully in the picture. The wags said this was the real reason Miranda didn't go to Detroit— that she hadn't become comfortable with Erica again and that Donáti couldn't take the two most-important women in his life sparring. One had to go, and Miranda was the one who bowed out.

Other speculators, pointing to the child, Alice, who had seemed to have just appeared backstage one day, opined that either the Donátis were not that pleased with Miranda with a child in tow or that, although refusing to even hint who the father was, Miranda felt she could not leave Washington, D.C., where the father lived.

Whatever the reason, Miranda transferred her miracle worker ways easily enough to the new conductor, Recevich. Since Miranda had first come to Washington with Donáti, the symphony had played in Constitutional Hall, the headquarters of the Daughters of the American Revolution, which, at the time, had the largest concert hall in the nation's capital. The Kennedy Center was built in 1986 and the symphony moved there. Miranda was never as comfortable at the new venue as she had been at the old, though, and she only stuck it out there for five more years, before, having recently learned that she was worth the millions her grandfather had left her, she was talking of retirement and looking for some appropriate, private and isolated, place to settle down. The Harrises had just moved to the smaller Washington village near the Blue Ridge in northern Virginia, and Angela found the castle, which was of elegant European design, something that pleased the international traveler, Miranda. So, taking her young teen daughter with her, and contracting to work checking orchestral compositions at home to fill in the time she didn't spend developing the castle's formal gardens, Miranda moved into Banffy.

As Ally lay there, slowly waking up to a new day in Angela Harris's guest bedroom, she entertained the question of her parentage for the first time in more than a year. She had no trouble deciding why she was bringing up the question now. She just didn't know why she hadn't given the likelihood greater consideration before. The previous day she had had two encounters with the past that linked in a way that was so obvious to her now that she was flabbergasted it hadn't occurred before.

August Donáti. It must have been August Donáti who had fathered her, despite his age at the time. Sixty-year-old men were known to be able to father children. Not that he'd ever been in a position to be more than biological contributor of the necessary material, of course. It was all so obvious now.

And what had triggered this revelation from the previous day's events? First had been those silver cups. The initials "A.D." on the cups. She had seen the initials before, and her mother's companion cup, but they had meant little to her. The previous day, in her mother's living room in the castle, though, had been the first time in many years that she remembered there was an inscription on the reverse side, "Forgotten Never." The initials, of course, were those of the conductor. And then there was the phonograph record Lois had given her from her mother—what had seemed to be Miranda's most precious possession when she was fleeing a burning building. August Donáti had been the conductor of the works on that record.

What would have been more natural in the 1975–76 time period? Her mother's whole life was devoted to August Donáti's needs. When would she have had time to meet another lover than the conductor? And because he was as old as he was and already in a longstanding marriage, of course he wouldn't have considered reordering his life to make a home with Miranda and her daughter. This even provided the best explanation of why Miranda had had the apparent falling out with the conductor's wife and hadn't gone with him to Detroit. There was a love child that the conductor and Miranda shared.

And August Donáti had been born and raised in Hungary—an Eastern Europe country.

Yes, it all fit into place. It perhaps should have lifted a great burden of doubt off Ally's shoulders to know the likelihood of this after all these years. But, strangely, it didn't. It didn't make her resent Donáti—certainly not in the vein that her mother resented all men. He had died in the late eighties, so there wasn't even any question of connecting with him after all these years. Erica was still alive—Angela got letters from her—but she wouldn't want to become any closer than that to her husband's love child either.

Still it was nice to have a mystery laid to rest—or at least that there was a rational explanation that could help her to stop speculating about her past. She hadn't really realized until now how much that question had weighed on her.

When Ally came down for breakfast, she found that Angela wasn't there. As the cook was bringing out a basket of warm rolls and an assortment of jellies, she said, "Mrs. Harris called while you were taking your shower. She has gone to Mrs. Aylor's farm and called when she got there and asked me to the tell you that this is one of your mother's good days, but that you should come over within an hour or two and plan not to stay too long. There is no telling how long her good day will last, and she tires so easily around strangers. Oh, excuse me. I didn't mean to put it that way."

"That's perfectly OK, Sally Ann," Ally quickly said. "I've been gone for several years and I'm afraid that I am a stranger to my mother now, with her condition and all. We'll try to fix that, but it's best I face the truth of it."

She was met at the door of Lois's house much as she had been the previous day, but this time Lois had a smile on her face that beamed from one ear to the other.

"Praise the Lord, this is one of her best days in weeks. And she knows you're coming. I don't think I'd mention that you were here yesterday, though. That is sure to confuse and worry her, and confusion is what sometimes makes her sink into herself."

"Of course. Thanks for mentioning it, Lois."

They moved down the front hall beside the staircase to the second level and toward the sunroom porch at the back of the house. Half way there, though, Lois, who was leading, stopped, turned to Ally, and laid a hand on her arm. "Mrs. Harris told me you showed her the phonograph record I gave you yesterday. It seemed to upset her a bit, and she said more than once that she hoped you wouldn't tell your mother you received that, so . . ."

"No, that's fine, Lois. I won't mention it."

Ten more steps and they were at the doorway of the sun porch, which was full of sunshine, and were standing in front of two women, holding hands and also looking radiant despite their ages. The two were sitting at the table facing the doorway.

The difference in the atmosphere on the porch between the previous day and this one was remarkable. There was a twinkle in the eyes of both Miranda and Angela. The two must have just recovered from having a good, shared laugh, and the faces of both lit up even more when they saw Ally at the door.

"Ally!" Miranda exclaimed, and Ally almost broke out in tears at the single word of recognition, imbued with love and welcome. "Come here and let me give you a hug, child."

Suddenly Ally was that child again, wanting nothing more than to be in her mother's comforting arms.

Angela sat, beaming and watching Ally come and lean down into her mother for an enveloping hug and a kiss on both cheeks.

"I didn't know what to expect. They'd told me you'd been badly injured and that there had been some surgeries—some reconstruction—but I can't see it, and you are beautiful. Even more beautiful than you ever were before."

"Most of the wounds are on the inside, Mother," Ally murmured. "We needn't dwell on those, but I would like to tell you about them." She started to cry—like she hadn't cried for anyone since the bombing. There was nothing like a mother's comfort. She started to whisper of all she had endured in the last several months and of the hurting she still felt, both in body and soul. She only spoke of Chad briefly, though, because she knew her mother wouldn't be pleased to hear about any men in her life.

Lois had brought a chair for her, and mother and daughter just sat side by side, in an embrace, while Miranda rocked her daughter back and forth and made calming noises at all Ally was telling her. Miranda's voice droned on in a murmur, telling her daughter repeatedly that everything would be OK.

And here, on this day, for the first time since she'd lost Chad and her body had been broken, Ally accepted that, yes, it would be OK. It wasn't OK right at this moment, but she had inherited the strength of her mother, and someday everything would be OK again.

* * * *

Sally Ann had driven Ally to Lois's farm on her way to the market, and Ally opted to walk back to Angela's house rather than wait for her in the car after the all-too-brief meeting with her mother in which Miranda seemed as lucid as ever. Angela had said it would be good for Ally not to stay too long the first time and for Angela to stay a few minutes longer to help calm Miranda down slowly.

The walk, which wasn't all that long a distance, was something Ally felt she needed to calm herself as well. She loved the small country village of Washington, often called Little Washington, to differentiate it from its much bigger brother up on the Potomac, Washington, D.C.. Founded in the mid eighteenth century and still a small village of no more than five blocks by two blocks, and having a population of about 150 permanent residents, the village had managed to remain quaint by playing on its favorable position in the shadow of the Blue Ridge Mountains and opening its well-preserved and maintained colonial buildings up as bed and breakfasts and high-end gift and antique stores.

The Inn at Little Washington held down the village's main intersection and kept the village on the "to see" map by maintaining its five-diamond/five-star hotel and dining room rating for probably longer than any other establishment in the greater Washington, D.C., region. The town was helped by all of the wealthy country estates in the surrounding area maintained by the important and rich of the nation's capital who wanted to live plantation style rather than in District of Colombia or northern Virginia or southern Maryland suburbs and high rises. The village was seventy miles in road-trip distance and about two hundred and fifty years in time from its bigger brother.

Ally hadn't made it into the center of the village from Lois's farm before a police cruiser pulled up beside her and Sheriff Shiflet leaned out of the side window, gave her a look that was a cross between a grimace and a sneer, and asked in a blustery voice, "Car trouble? Need a lift to somewhere?"

"No thanks, sheriff," Ally answered, not stopping, but slowing down. Shiflet's car was keeping pace with her. "I've just been to Lois Aylor's farm to visit my mother, and I'm walking back into town. I'm staying with Angela Harris."

"Seeing your mother, eh? And staying at the Harrises'? So you've decided not to stay up at the castle?"

"Not for a while at least. Angela's an old friend. We have a lot of catching up to do."

"Given thought to the need to tear the place up there down? As I said, the judge won't wait long to give an order himself, and you very well could end up spending more to get it done on his schedule."

"No, I'm still thinking that one out." Ally didn't know why she didn't tell the sheriff straight out that she'd decided to take on the restoration of the castle as a project. He just seemed much too anxious for her to tear it down, and he irritated her.

"It would be best all the way around. And your mother could go into a home somewhere away from here."

"Sheriff, I really don't think . . ." She was having a hard time completing that sentence. He was being entirely too pushy. She hadn't even thought of taking her mother away from here.

"Yep, best for all, I suppose," he continued. "It would stop a lot of talk, it would. A lot of talk about your mother and those missing men. Probably the best way to protect her."

"I hardly think my mother needs protection," Ally retorted, finding it very hard now not to show how steamed she was. "And I'm surprised that law enforcement pays that much attention to malicious rumors."

"OK, Ms. Templeton. You have a nice day now. And I'd give it all a little thought, if I was you."

With that, the sheriff picked up speed with his cruiser and made a smooth left-hand turn at the inn's intersection, without even hesitating at the four-way stop sign, and was gone from Ally's view.

The tension he had brought to her hadn't gone away by the time she reached Angela's house. She was fumbling with the key in the lock on the front door until she realized the door wasn't locked and remembered that Angela had told her there wasn't much locking of doors in the village. Without really giving it much thought, she went straight for her cell phone and rang through to one of her colleagues at the State Department in D.C.'s Foggy Bottom district.

"Hello, Rachel? It's Ally. Ally Templeton. Yes, fine, thank you. Glad to be back. Yes, I'll be here in Little Washington for a while. Say, I'm calling because I wondered if you might do me a favor . . . yes, just checking with anyone you can rustle up in our embassy in Prague. Could you ask someone there to check on whether a symphony violinist, Dennis Harris . . . yes, an old friend of my mothers. You remember she was the conductor's assistant at the National Symphony. Could you ask for an advisory on whether Dennis Harris is living in Prague? No, not a great hurry. But I'll call you back at the end of the week, if you don't mind. Yes, the mountains are restful. Just what I need for now. Yes, every day in every way I'm healing a bit more, Thanks. No, I don't know when I'll be back at work."

After a few more pleasantries, she rang off and flopped down in one of the overstuffed chairs in Angela's parlor. She had no idea why she'd done that, she thought. But then she thought the contrary. These rumors had to stop. She'd trace down all four of the men people claimed had mysteriously disappeared after having fights. Dennis was the easiest to start with. She'd find where they all were, and then people would have to stop talking—and that Sheriff Shiflet would have to wipe that accusing smirk off his face.

* * * *

"If it was me—and especially if you intend to restore the whole place—I wouldn't just make do with a ceiling in this tower room. There's four flights inside these stone tower walls. I'd do it all at once, put in the flooring for three stories and a staircase going all the way up. That way you'd have it done once and for all and would gain four weather-tight rooms here. The three upper floors could be used to store smaller construction material until it was needed and then finished off as rooms when the rest was done."

"That's probably a good idea," Ally responded to Jake. "Give me an estimate on that, please—if you're interested in subcontracting for that project."

Ally and the contractor with the red truck, Jake Monroe, were doing a walking survey of the main part of the castle. He was helping Ally decide what should be done first and was taking notes on what part of the subcontract he wanted to bid on.

"Come into the ballroom next," Ally said. "There's some tearing out to be done there before any construction can be done."

"The ballroom? There was a ballroom here?"

"Yes, nearly this whole side of the main central core was one long room. We were using it as a living room in good weather. That circular tower alcove over there was our music room. I see that mother had the room partitioned off since I lived here last. Maybe she had you put in this wall and these bookcase units? You said you'd done construction work for her."

"Not that I remember," Jake answered. "So, you say this was one long room at one time, that this wall wasn't here with book and display cases opening to each of the smaller rooms?"

"Yes. And a grand ballroom it was. Higher ceilings than other rooms. created by sinking the floor by several steps. I'd like to put it back to exactly the way it was. Do you think you can handle the work?"

"Most of it, I think. You sure you want to do that with these rooms, though? They'd look great the way they are with a little refurbishing. That thick wall between them, with built-in bookcases and display cases on either side was really well done. I'd be sorry to see that torn out. And the two rooms would seem more useful than one big one. Unless you're planning to have balls up here, of course."

"Hardly that," Ally answered, with a laugh. "But I really was thinking of a total restoration. I'll have to think about that." She had no intention of thinking about that, but she didn't want to argue with the man. Although she found him very attractive, he didn't seem to be the type of man who gave much credence to a woman on construction issues.

"Please do. Great proportions in these rooms now. And back on the job contracting part. My crew wouldn't be able to do the electrical work. That was my brother, Craig's, part, and he's not here anymore. I haven't been able to replace him and just subcontract that part. I've got someone in mind. I can send him up here someday soon that you know you'll be here. How would that be?"

"Sounds great. Does it look like too big a job, Jake?" Ally asked, giving him a concerned look and willing him to say it would all be fine.

"If you've got the money, I'm sure it can be done," he said. "And as long as you have time to give it. I'm not so sure about you thinking you can be the contractor and subcontracting parts out, but that can always change when and if you decide it's too much."

"There's money," Ally said. "And right at the moment all I can see stretching in front of me for months and months is time. I think it will be good for me to have a big, complex project like this to work on. So, what were you thinking about a staircase in the tower back in my mother's rooms?" There it was, straight

87

away. She was mere woman and he was "the man." She almost regretted that she found him so physically appealing.

"It's getting dark and running up to time for us to be getting off the mountain," Jake said. "How about me taking you to dinner and we can discuss the tower plans over a good meal."

"Dinner? You're asking me to dinner?" Her instincts told her she should say no, but this was the first time since Chad had been lost that she had thought of man in terms of physical attraction.

"Yes, of course. This is a big job you got here. If I get a lot of the subcontracts we're probably going to be having a lot of construction planning meetings over a dinner."

"But I'm not dressed for it. The only place I know of nearby is the inn, and I'm certainly not dressed for that. We could stop at Angela Harris's house and I could—"

"You look fine—in fact you look great to me—even for the inn. But there's another place where the food is nearly as good and the dress code is more sensible for the country. In fact, there are several really good country restaurants around here. But the one I have in mind is in Flint Hill—just about a fifteen-minute ride from Washington back toward Front Royal. It's called the Public House. How about we go there?"

"Well, OK, I guess that will work."

Was this a date? Ally wondered. Could she trust herself on a date with Jake Monroe? He was quite a man, but was she really ready to start getting involved with anyone this soon? There was another reason she should go with him. He'd mentioned his brother, Craig. Yet another one of the guys she needed to track down to scotch the rumors about her mother and disappearing men. She should be able to find a way of discovering where this brother had gone, if Jake knew. And she did have to eat. She'd told Angela she wouldn't be at her place for dinner, thinking that this walk-through would have been over long before it was and that she'd go over the mountain into Harrisonburg for dinner and to check on a lumber yard she had heard was there and would be a reasonably priced supplier for her construction needs. Jake's sensitivities notwithstanding, she already was thinking like a contractor.

As it turned out, though, the occasion hadn't arisen during the dinner in Flint Hill for her to subtly ask Jake about his brother and where he might be. Jake had wanted to spend most of the time over dinner talking about Ally and where she'd been in the world and what she'd seen. And she'd fallen for his charm. It was all she could do not to let him charm the pants off her—if that's what he had in mind.

Half way through the meal Ally stopped and gave an embarrassed little laugh. "But listen to me. I've done nothing but talk for the better part of the meal. I haven't let loose like this with a stranger for some time."

"Well, I hope we won't be strangers," he had answered, giving her a warm smile. "And I could listen to you for hours. Has anyone ever told you that you had the voice of a Kathleen Turner? So sensually rich, putting people at ease."

Ally blushed—and not just at the use of the word "sensually." They'd both had a hand on the table top, and she thought she would have left it there if Jake had covered her hand with his at that moment. She was pleased at the comparison. Yes, she had rather thought herself that she sounded like Kathleen Turner—even that she looked a bit like her. And it pleased her to no end whenever someone else noticed that and remarked on it. And beyond that, even though she'd told Jake something about the bombing in Amman—without mentioning Chad, of course— never during the afternoon or night had Jake remarked on the burn marks on her left arm.

So, in the end, the topic of Jake's missing brother, Craig, hadn't come up.

But even if Jake had kept the evening from going anywhere near there, she had to admit that she hadn't enjoyed an evening with anyone, man or woman, since Chad had been in her life like she enjoyed this evening with Jake.

Chapter Five: Grizzly Find

What Angela had to say to Ally at breakfast in the morning two weeks later hit her doubly hard because of the telephone call she made before coming down to breakfast in order to get through to Europe while the embassies there were still open. She already was in a melancholy and edgy mood, because, although Miranda had recognized her on a few visits—not more than half of them, though—she had not again been as demonstrative toward Ally as on that first meeting of recognition. It seemed that, having done her duty of acknowledging that Ally was back home and in need of repair herself, Miranda had drawn away from her.

The first blow came in the call to the U.S. embassy in Prague, to the Foreign Service officer Ally's colleague at the State Department had put her in contact with.

"Yes, Ms. Templeton, we did do an extensive search. If the man you're seeking, Dennis Harris, is practicing his musical profession here at all, he just isn't coming up on our radar. And we have no one by that name listed in the American expatriate community either."

This was the opposite of what Ally wanted to hear—had assumed she'd hear. Rumors were floating on where Dennis Harris had gone after a big fight with Miranda. Angela said he was living in Prague now and playing his violin with orchestras. But Ally wasn't able to find him. Angela was Miranda's best friend in the world. They frequently said they'd do anything for each other. Ally was worried that their pledge had been sorely tested.

Ally went to breakfast determined to pin Angela down on exactly where Dennis Harris was. Angela beat her to the punch though, on dropping a bombshell.

"Ally," she said as Ally entered the dining room a sat at the table. "There's been something eating at me that I've meant to tell you ever since you came back."

"Yes?" Ally asked. Here it is, Ally thought. She didn't have to pursue the "where is Dennis?" question. Angela was going to spill the beans on this under her own steam.

"I'm sure you were wondering why I was denying Miranda the comforts of my home when she's in this state. Me living here all alone in this big house—all alone when I've been your mother's closest friend for decades."

"No, I haven't, really," Ally answered, somewhat confused, because, in fact, she had given it a thought initially and then had let it slip her mind when perhaps she should have given

92

it greater thought. It hadn't seemed more than a curiosity, but now that Angela mentioned it, it did seem significantly odd.

"Lois explained that well enough to me. Mother is used to having Lois in the house with her, and Lois is trained to work with dementia patients. This arrangement also, I know, is a way to supplement Lois's income. Lois has been with mother so long, she deserves a pension from her. Those all seem like good reasons to me for mother to be with Lois."

"Ah, well. I'm glad to know it hasn't been concerning you. I assure you that it has concerned me and that I'd like nothing better than to have Miranda here with me. But . . . but, I think perhaps for other reasons I should go ahead and explain myself on this."

"Yes, of course, if you wish."

"I will flat out and say it. We made a pact long ago, Miranda and I did, that if either of us got in a state like Miranda is in, the other would help her pass on."

The bald statement of it—the natural logic of it that somehow had totally escaped Ally—took Ally's breath away momentarily.

"You and mother made an assisted death compact?" There it was, the pledge to do anything at all for each other.

"Yes. She's the one who pushed for it, but we made it at a time when my own mother was slowly dying from a stroke and I was determined I'd never let myself linger like that. But I never thought it would come to this. I'm the elder and have always been

93

the one with more health problems. I assumed I would be the first one to go—and I've grown to give no credence to it anyway. Unfortunately, your mother, in her lucid moments, seems to be serious about this agreement."

"You are saying she wants you to arrange for her death?"

"Yes, I'm afraid so. On that basis, I almost welcome my visits with her when she is not quite lucid enough to raise the issue with me. It's a very private matter between the two of us. As far as I know, you are the only other person who has ever been told. I think I can cope with it just by visiting with her—I usually check with Lois and don't go over on one of her more aware days. I know your mother wouldn't say anything to Lois about it, but if I were there . . ."

"If you were there and she was fully lucid, she would be after you to carry through on the agreement. And if she lived here with you, there would be more of those moments, and they possibly would be more intense."

"Yes, that's exactly right. I'm glad that you see that. So, that's why I keep her, shall we say, a bit compartmentalized and mostly there rather than here."

"And you don't think you could help her in that way?"

"I keep struggling with it, but no, not now, at least. She seems comfortable, and when she isn't lucid, she isn't worrying or depressed. So, not now, no. And if the time did come, I'm not sure I'd be up to it. And I'm afraid it's tearing me apart. I don't want her to leave life thinking that I've let her down. But I don't want to live my life knowing that I took the life of my best friend, either."

And now it will tear me apart too, Ally thought. What she said, though, was, "Yes, I understand. I'm really sorry that your relationship has come down to this perplexity."

"I'm mainly sorry that your mother has come to this point. But you know the steel she has in her back. I don't think she's going to change her mind. Especially now."

"Especially now?"

"Yes. She had been saying that she had nothing else to be here for except for you to be home again. I'm afraid that she saw your intended marriage as an impediment to that. And now that you are home . . . and not married. I'm afraid she's said she thought you would be better off single."

"I noticed that our closeness hasn't built since that first meeting I had with her when she was fully lucid. So, you're telling me that she now wants to go—and wants you to arrange that?" Ally also was thinking that now she had to bear the responsibility of bringing this all to a head.

"Yes, I'm afraid so. When she's aware enough to talk to me about it, I try to keep Lois in the room with us as much as possible. She won't broach the subject while Lois is in the room."

"You mentioned depression, and Lois has told me that depression helps bring the effects of dementia on. Do you think there is anything we can do to lessen her depression at this point?"

"I've thought about that. The only thing I can think of is getting her out of the house occasionally. Taking her for rides, maybe even up to the castle so she can see that you are fixing it up. But it's not something I could do unless I took Lois with us, and I don't know how I would explain to Lois that she should go with us rather than have the time away from your mother to have a rest and to do what she'd like to do."

"I guess I can try to do that to see if it helps. But what if she—?"

"I don't think she would ask you to help her pass. I just don't think Miranda would ask that of you."

Angela, having already finished her breakfast, rose then and left Ally to begin eating hers. It wasn't until Ally was on the road in her BMW convertible—its delivery a symbol of her decision that she was staying here for a prolonged period—that Ally realized that Angela's revelation had completely knocked any thoughts of Dennis Harris from her mind.

Events later in the day were to force that question even deeper into the recesses of her brain.

* * * *

There was so much to think of now, plans to make, care to take, as Ally drove up to the castle, past the Mountain Castle vineyards, that she wasn't really all that aware of her surroundings until she cleared the stands of vines and entered the newly mown slopes of the castle's front lawn. She had contracted with a landscaping company to keep that cut down as a first assault on the garden. The more extensive, once-formal gardens at the other side of the castle would have to wait until later—probably much later.

The first thing she saw when she entered her own property was the old silver Airstream trailer off to the side near the edge of the woods. She frowned, not liking the look of it, and how she had just fallen into letting it be there. It was in excellent condition, considering how old it must be, but it still looked very much out of place to her. She had looked in that direction because she still was distressed at seeing the condition of the castle when she drove up to it. Improvements already were being made, but not to any area that could be seen from the frontal approach.

The old yellow truck that went with the Airstream wasn't there, so Hugh Coles must not be on the property. Ally felt a twinge of disappointment, but she was a little irritated that she did.

She still felt duped by and at odds with Hugh. He seemed so easygoing and amenable, and yet he always seemed to get his way. They would argue, never seriously, and have differences of opinion, which somehow would be resolved as Hugh had proposed but with Ally being left to feel that she had forced that very decision, with Hugh acquiescing to her opinion. It didn't help that when he made a suggestion about what she needed to do with a construction project, he always seemed to be right. He'd been hired just for the electrician duties, and yet he commented on other aspects of the restoration as well. He was just so charming and always with the gentle joke, though. At least that's how Ally saw it. She could see that Jake Monroe took Hugh's comments with a great deal more irritation.

The hiring of Hugh had been a fluke and had created some resentment among the crew Ally had put together to get started on the restoration. Jake had told her that his crew didn't do electrical work and that he had someone he'd send up to talk to Ally about subcontracting with her for that. So, Ally wasn't surprised when, working alone packing up what could be salvaged of her mother's things to store them away until those rooms were redone, she heard a car horn beeping at the front of the building.

"Hello, ma'am," a tall, slender young man of maybe thirty, with reddish-blond hair, a sheepish smile, and wearing a Georgia Tech T-shirt above worn jeans and sandals without socks, said to her as she appeared in the doorway. He tipped his baseball cap off his head, which Ally was rarely to see off his head, bill pointed to the back, from then on out.

"Yes, may I help you?" Beyond him was parked a sixties-vintage pickup truck that once had been a bright sunshine color but was now mostly gray matte paint encroaching from everywhere on a base of tired, faded yellow.

"I hope so, ma'am. I heard you might need some help up here—that you were restoring this castle."

"I'm trying to, yes."

"And doing the contracting yourself." It was more a statement than a question, and Ally steeled herself to get the same attitude and lip she was getting from most of the men in the construction industry she'd had to deal with so far—that contracting wasn't something she was going to be able to do. That it was not proper work for a woman, and especially not a "city girl."

She simply gave him a terse nod.

"Good for you," he said. "And good that you're restoring this beauty. There are those who would tear it down and put up a Lindal cedar house, I'm sure. But I think this is a perfect place for it. It should be everyone's fairytale dream."

Perhaps it was at this moment that no matter how Ally occasionally got irritated by this guy, he was in as a subcontractor if he specialized in anything she needed.

"I'm Hugh Coles. I'm a certified electrician. Got papers if you want to see them. From what I see, your first problem is that the line is down over there near the trees. That's the first thing that needs to be done, to get the line back up to the house. Now if you don't have an electrician yet, I'd start with that. If you do, you might want to look into why he didn't start with that."

"When could you start?"

"Right this instant, if you want. Or near enough."

"Well, let's go inside and we'll talk about what there is and we can set on the fees—and, yes, I'll need to see your certification." Almost as an afterthought, as they were walking into the central foyer, she said. "I guess Jake Monroe sent you up."

Rather than answering that, Hugh said, "I've got a trailer I can live in. If you don't mind and would like to get the job done sooner and have a watchman on the property at night, I could pull my trailer up here and put it over there away from your buildings."

"Why, I don't know. I suppose—"

"Once you get a lot of construction material up here, you're going to have to worry about vandals. You'll need someone on the property at night."

"I plan to have some rooms set up and live here from the early stages of restoration myself, but that can't be for a couple of weeks I suppose. So, I guess . . ."

"Well, OK, I'll be back in a bit and we can talk specifics then."

She was quickly and effectively trapped then—or at least felt the decision was made for her. He wasn't gone in his truck more than ten minutes before he was coming back up onto the property with an Airstream in tow. He couldn't have had it parked much farther down the road than just beyond where the stands of grape vines started.

He was out and already working on restringing the line to the castle over at the service entrance side when Jake Monroe drove up in his red truck with another man. The testiness started when Ally discovered that this was the electrician Jake was bringing to talk to her, not Hugh Coles.

Coles was already on the job, though; they had agreed on fees that Ally thought were quite acceptable; and Coles's certification for Virginia was established and he even showed her proof of an engineering degree from Georgia Tech. So, having made no commitment to Jake, Ally couldn't see a justification for switching gears. In the subsequent week and a half, Jake, who Ally was led to suspect would have been given a kickback from the other electrician if he'd been signed on, only spoke to Hugh when necessary, while Hugh always responded cheerfully as if nothing at all was wrong. Of course, Ally got the impression that some of the suggestions Hugh made on the construction work were said just to irritate Jake and that Hugh went out of his way to needle the older man. The two obviously had taken an instant dislike to each other.

On this morning, as she drove up to the building, Ally wondered why Hugh's truck wasn't there. He had always been somewhere around in the morning at least until other construction workers had arrived. He took his watchman duties seriously. She didn't have long to think about this, though, as Jake was rolling up the hill in his red truck.

Jake and Ally started off the morning with the same running argument they had been engaged in from the previous evening. Ally was saying it was time to take down the bookcase wall that was partitioning off the ballroom, and Jake was dragging his feet, making the argument that it was best the way it was and that the wall was too nice to take down. To Ally's chagrin, Hugh was agreeing with Jake on this.

They started in what had been Miranda's living quarters, though, on which work had begun on the fire damage. The three levels of flooring inside the tower and the staircase going up to the fourth level, with a narrower staircase there going up to a trapdoor that led to the tower battlements, had been completed, and Jake was ready to move on to something else.

"Yes, Jake the tower structure is very nice. But now I'd like the walls taken out of the rest of the first floor that aren't in the original plans."

"Don't you want us to finish off the rooms you want to occupy while the construction is going on?" he countered. It was an old argument now. He was dragging his feet on getting into the central section of the building. Again.

Before she could answer, he continued. "I've got to go down into Luray before my crew's ready to come up this morning. There's some building supplies I want them to truck up. You think about where you want to move next while I'm gone."

I've thought about where I want to move next already, Ally thought, fuming. But Jake liked to treat her like she was his pupil rather than his boss—the contractor—so she said nothing. She just stood there, by the gaping opening of one of the tall windows from the old ballroom area out onto the front lawn of the castle.

She watched Jake get in his truck and drive down the road. When the tail end of his truck disappeared into the sea of grape vine stands, she calmly walked over to the side of the room, where she'd put a sledge hammer the night before. Then she walked to the finely fitted book case wall in the partition that made the old ballroom into two rooms. She stood there and looked at the wall for a couple of minutes. She had to agree that the workmanship had been excellent, even though she had no idea who had done the work and when.

And then she lifted the sledgehammer, swung it way back and then forward, connecting with the wood of the bookcases. And started to destroy the wall. This would decide the issue forever. When Jake got back, the wall would be so destroyed that there would be no question that the partition was going.

It wasn't more than twenty minutes before she was breaking through from the bookcases on one side to the bookcases on the other side. She'd moved to a flush panel where a picture had hung and the electrical switches and outlets were located. The flush wall was about three feet wide. When she'd checked the other side, that section of wall was flush to the front of the bookcases there too. So, there were ducts or something back there. This perplexed her. There were no air conditioning ducts and the heat ducks should be on the side walls, because this partition was an addition, and it wasn't a load-bearing wall.

She took three good, solid swings at that section of the wall. She was raring back for a really strong swing, having broken through the wall with the previous swing, when she looked at the wall, dropped the sledgehammer dangerously close to her foot, and let out a scream.

The skull of the corpse that was wedged inside the wall was staring back at her with what seemed to be a hideous grin on its face.

Ally leaned over and vomited, and then she backed away from the wall several paces, one scream fading into the renewal of the next one. She turned and stumbled back through the central foyer and toward the back of the castle. When she cleared the building, she started into a panicked run through the overgrown back gardens, striking out toward the safety of the woods. Once inside the shade of the forest, she continued to dodge from tree to tree, moving uphill, putting as much distance between her and the castle as possible.

Her foot caught on the root of a tree at the edge of a clearing and she sprawled, heavily on the ground. The pain of her turned ankle broke through the haze of her shock, and she rolled over and sat up, rubbing her ankle and cursing.

She found she was staring into the face of Sheriff Ed Shiflet. He was dressed in camouflage hunting gear and was standing, staring in paralyzed surprise at the unceremonious arrival of the unexpected figure. He was holding some sort of iron implement in his hand, almost brandishing it like a weapon, and was planted firmly in front of what obviously was a puffing-away whiskey still.

* * * *

"Listen, Sheriff Shiflet," Ally said wearily as she sat, swathed in a blanket and steaming cup of coffee in hand, on the tailgate of an ambulance in the front court of the castle, "I don't care about whatever is going on up there in the woods. What I care about is who that is who is in that wall in my house and why."

Shiflet sighed a sigh of relief. Ally thought she understood now why he'd been so anxious for her just to tear the castle ruins down and sell the land off to the national park system. It looked an awful lot like the sheriff was using his position to cover a salary-augmenting illegal activity and wanted to do it as far away from anyone's house as he could. But she was serious; ferreting out and turning in moonshiners in Virginia just wasn't on her "to do" list. If she wanted to do that here in these mountains, it probably would be a full-time job and most likely would entail being willing to swallow a good bit of buckshot.

"You say that you want to help pursue this no matter where it leads? This is your mother's house, and you know about the rumors about her and men. That body is at least partly mummified, having been in a dry, confined cavity like that. There's no telling how long it's been there. Cooperating will mean I've gotta talk to your mother and she's gonna need to answer some questions."

"Good luck talking to my mother, sheriff. She has dementia—you should know she has that and that she isn't faking it. Her lucid days are getting to be fewer and fewer. I have no fears of you looking into her activities when she lived up here, though. I know she couldn't have been any part of this." She was speaking with more bravery than she felt. Her thoughts went back to Dennis Harris and why she couldn't locate him in Prague, where Angela had said he'd gone. She had to remember to pin Angela down on that.

"I'll give you all the help I can. And for starters, I can give you a 'no-earlier-than' date for the body being put in that wall."

"Yeah? What would that be."

"That wall wasn't there seven years ago when I was last home," Ally answered. "That's why I was knocking it down. I'm restoring the castle to its original form. That wall divides what was the original ballroom. So, the body couldn't have been put in there earlier than that."

"Well, now, that does help," the Sheriff said. "So your mother can tell me when that wall went in?"

"If she remembers and understands the question in her condition," Ally answered.

"And if not, there are records of the construction here— receipts and such?"

"Probably burned up in the last fire here," Ally said. Looking toward the façade of the castle, she saw that Jake Monroe had returned and was talking with some of the forensic

106

technicians who were still going back and forth into the castle ruins. "There's Jake Monroe over there, though," she said to the sheriff. "He's done construction here before. I asked him earlier about the wall and he said it wasn't his company's work, but maybe he can help you pin down when it was done and who did it."

"Good possibility," Shiflet said. He tipped his hat in the closest to an act of respect he was going to give, but the look he gave Ally indicated a deeper appreciation for an entirely different kindness she was giving him. Then he strode off to talk with Jake.

Ally watched them talking animatedly across the yard, taking the time alone to try to calm her shaking and regain her composure. Finding the body in the wall had really rattled her, and while she'd been escaping from the scene, she'd been hyperventilating and in a panic that she now felt was way out of proportion to the situation. As she thought about that now, she realized it had been a release of fear and grief that she hadn't yet let loose of in the wake of Chad's death. Perhaps this would help her cope with the terrorist incident and start to heal. What worse could happen now? But then she thought of her mother and the danger she was in from this, and her hand holding the coffee cup began to shake again.

Shiflet came back to her. "Jake was only able to help a bit," he said as he reached her. "He said the wall was there when his company did some work here three years ago—after a fire.

You have had quite a few fires here, it seems. Sort of suspicious, that."

"My mother smoked in bed," Ally responded. "More to the point, she had a habit of lighting up in bed and then getting up for one of her nocturnal wanderings and leaving the cigarette to start a fire. I suppose it's a blessing that she was never in the bed herself when the flames started."

"Ah. He told me something else as well. He says that Hugh Cole has been doing electrical work here too."

"Yes, he has. You know Hugh? I thought he'd just recently come up from Georgia."

"Just up from Georgia? He tell you that?"

"No, not in so many words. Hugh hasn't said much to me about his past at all. His credentials were good, though."

"They better be good," Shiflet said with a laugh. "The dude's got a doctorate in electrical engineering."

"A doctorate? The only evidence he showed me was a bachelor's degree."

"Yep, an engineering doctorate. I thought he'd be off teaching at some university now. He's from these parts—well, over the mountain from here. Jake says he's even already done some work on this place. He came back here summers during college and got in with a really rough crowd. He comes from the Luray area, but I guess he didn't want them over there to see what a hell raiser he was, so he brought his business over here. I was zeroing in on him when he up and left and went back to Georgia Tech to work on his doctorate."

"When was he here?"

"Last here about five years ago, as I recall. Jake seems to think he was working on your mother's place when he up and left—that he and she had some sort of row."

"Oh," Ally said, fighting hard not to show her concern at this revelation.

"Yep, 'oh' would be just about right. Your mom seemed to have a big fight with just about every man she met."

Just about, at least in later years, Ally thought. But, of course, she wasn't going to give the sheriff any ammunition she didn't have to.

Shiflet took up the conversation again. "It would really be nice to know who that is in the wall. And we should be able to find that out after the medical examiner has had a go at the body. But it would be double nice to wrap this one up before those results are in. I think I want to talk to Hugh Coles fast like. Is he supposed to show up here pretty soon?"

"He should be here now. He's staying in the old Airstream trailer over there by the trees. He's working as the night watchman too. He wasn't here when I came up here this morning, though, I don't think. His truck was gone."

"What Airstream? I don't see an Airstream over there."

Alley turned her face toward where the trailer should be. It was gone.

Chapter Six: It's News

Ally sat by her mother on Lois's sun porch, holding Miranda's hands in hers and talking soothingly to her. Angela was hovering nearby. Lois and Sheriff Shiflet were concealed in the hallway just beyond the sun porch door, where they could hear but couldn't be seen.

It was no use, however. Miranda had recognized her daughter when she came in, Angela already having been there and prepared her friend for the visit. But the more Ally gently tried to draw information about the past from her mother, the more glassy-eyed and withdrawn into some world of her own Miranda became.

"The ballroom, Mother. You remember that nice ballroom in the castle. And how you had it partitioned off . . ."

Ally just stopped there, seeing that there was no use going on. Miranda wasn't agitated and she was still smiling, but she just wasn't there anymore.

"Perhaps if you took her up there and let her see what you're doing at the castle, she'll remember more," Angela said in a quiet voice.

"That could work, yes," Ally said. "But you saw her reaction when I brought the subject up. Or rather her nonreaction. She isn't disturbed by the question. There's no fear in her awareness about the ballroom and the partitioning of that room. And I brought it up without preliminary warning. You saw her face when I introduced the topic, didn't you?"

Ally wasn't looking at Angela when she said this; she was looking toward the door to the hallway. And she had lifted her voice. Angela caught the drift and she used a louder voice too that would clearly convey to the ears of the sheriff where he was standing just on the other side of the doorway.

"Yes, I saw. The topic didn't seem to disturb her at all. If anything she seemed pleased that you were talking about the castle. You had said you thought that taking her out occasionally might lessen her depression and therefore sharpen her awareness, so, yes, it's certainly worth a try."

Ally left Miranda with Angela after saying good-bye to her mother and went out into the hall. Lois slipped past her onto the sun porch, and Ally walked the sheriff to his cruiser out in front of the house.

"I don't think she's holding anything back, and I'm trying to get answers—truthful answers—from her," Ally said as they reached the car.

"Yes, I can see that. And you're sure there are no records around on the construction documents?"

"I haven't found any in the castle, and I'm not aware of any storage unit she has about. I've checked our safety deposit box at the bank and haven't found anything. As far as I know, the only box she has at a bank is our shared one. Mother would have kept all of the paperwork, but there have been fires in her living area in the castle. Chances are good all of her papers on construction projects went up in smoke."

"But you'll try taking her to the scene and seeing if that will jog her memory?"

"Yes, of course. I'll take her for a few rides in the countryside and maybe to Angela's for a visit first to see how well outings set with her. But I'll get her up to the castle as soon as I can. What about the identification of the body? Won't it help a lot to know who died?"

"Yes, of course it will. But the medical examiner was only willing to tell me that it was a male. Old Horace keeps his cards close to his chest; he stays well this side of speculation. All he would tell me other than that was that he had sent stuff off to the lab. He doesn't think we'll get anything back on that for a couple of weeks. The findings will have to go from the lab to the State police to see if an identification can be established."

"OK. In the meantime I'll try again to coax something out of my mother."

"I'll be in my office all afternoon in case you think of anything that will help," the sheriff said, as he muscled his bulk behind the steering wheel of the car. Neither one of them had said a word about Ally having stumbled across him at the mountain still, and, as long as it was making the sheriff a whole lot nicer to her and standoffish on Miranda, Ally would just leave it that way.

Lois was at the door when the sheriff had driven off toward Washington and Ally came back up the walk.

"I'm not sure what all of the fuss is about," Lois said as she stepped back and Ally entered the house. "I don't like Miranda being upset like this."

"Upset? Do you think Mother was upset by my asking her those questions?" Lois knew Miranda's reactions better than anyone. If Lois thought that the questions about the partition in the ballroom had been upsetting to Miranda . . .

"No, not by you or anything you asked her. But that sheriff. First thing Miranda did when she knew he was gone was to ask for a cigarette. And she only does that when she's been agitated. He'd intimidate almost anyone. He certainly scared the stuffing out of my Felix."

"Yes, he would," Ally said, with a little laugh. "But he stayed out of sight in the hallway. I'm sure Mother didn't even know he was here."

"Well, I suppose not . . . but I knew he was here, and I don't know what the fuss is all about. So they found a body in a wall in the castle. What does that have to do with my missy down here in my house?"

"Don't you listen to the village rumors, Lois?"

"Not if I can help it. And I don't contribute to them either. Let me make that darn well sure."

"Of course, Lois. But mother's name has been connected with fighting with various men, and the men then disappearing soon thereafter. One of those men was your husband, Felix. So, when a body is found in the wall in her house . . . well, it could be your own husband, you know. It could be Felix who was walled up in the castle. I thought you would have considered that possibility. And there's that mountain man who was bothering her up at the castle for a while and then just stopped coming around after she'd gone after him with a broom."

"My Felix? Up there in Ms. Templeton's wall?" Lois snorted and then gave a dry laugh. Ally shot her a sharp look.

"You think that's funny—or not possible? I assure you that suspicion is laying on Mother over this. The sheriff isn't the least of those who is suspicious."

"Funny and not possible both," Lois said. "And your mother knows it." She paused, though, and her face took on a more serious look. "Of course I guess there's no reason anyone else knows it—probably including Mrs. Harris. I told you I don't gossip. And neither does your mother. But maybe one or both of us should have paid a bit more attention to the gossip and nipped it in the bud."

"I don't understand," Ally said.

"My Felix—and that drifter, Hank Morris who bothered your mother—I can tell you that it was because he was sweet on her, and I don't have to tell you that she wasn't sweet on him—ain't dead. I knew that, and so does your mother, when her memory isn't on the fritz. My Felix has created a different family from me and is living in Lynchburg—with another wife. And she's welcome to him, thank you very much. In fact he already was living with both her and me when your mother got wind of it and gave the deadbeat a tongue lashing that sent him all the way down to Lynchburg for good. And as for Hank Morris, he gave up on your mother and got sweet on some woman over in Luray. All of his jaunts out of the secret hollow of his in the mountains are out on the other side of the Blue Ridge now. And it's a good riddance to him too."

"They are alive? They can be contacted?" Ally asked in disbelief.

"Yep, always could have. All folks need to have done is ask—or done a little checkin' themselves. Your mother and me just didn't think it was anybody else's business."

"God, Lois, that's great news," Ally gushed. "Where's your telephone? The sheriff said he'd be at his office all this afternoon. This cuts the field considerably. You've got to tell him what you know and tell him where he can contact these two."

"Um, OK," Lois said, still not completely getting it.

"Don't you understand, Lois? The sheriff is including those two as possible identification for the body taken from the castle. If he can eliminate these two, that will help the investigation—and it will also take some of the cloud of suspicion from over Mother's head."

This development didn't fully solve Ally's fears, though. The body still could be that of Dennis Harris, although she wasn't about to offer that possibility to anyone. If that was the identification, she would like it to be one made by the medical examiner and the police.

"Oh, I see," Lois exclaimed. And she was off double time for the telephone hanging on the wall in her kitchen.

* * * *

The morning had gone well. It had been a week and a half since the body had been found in the ballroom wall. Nothing had transpired on that investigation. Ally was still waiting for an identification of the body. If the authorities knew anything on that front, they were keeping it to themselves. But the sheriff's department wasn't bugging either Ally or, through her, Miranda hard. Lois's revelation that not all men Miranda had chewed out in the last five years had disappeared had taken the edge off that rumor.

Miranda hadn't really become lucid enough to ask about the partition construction, but she seemed to be improving a bit, helped, everyone thought, by the short trips away from Lois's farm. Ally had checked every other day on Miranda's condition, and if she showed any spark of recognition of the world surrounding her, Ally took her someplace for a short excursion. They'd been for drives through the village of Washington and then to Flint Hill to the northeast. They'd been up on the Skyline Drive, where they sat on the stone wall at an overlook and ate ham sandwiches and watched life go on in the valley below. And just this morning they'd driven over to Angela's house for tea. That had gone so well that Ally might have extended their stay if she didn't have to go across the mountain to negotiate a bill with a lumber supplier in the Shenandoah Valley town of Luray.

Ally thought that the next outing could be up to the castle. She was looking forward to that both with the hope that it would bring Miranda back closer to reality and with trepidation that it could push her deeper into depression.

Hugh Coles hadn't returned with his Airstream and the sheriff was still looking for him. When Ally asked the sheriff if he'd found Hugh yet, Shiflet had just muttered and said something about folks in Luray knowing something but stonewalling him. Ally couldn't help but feel relieved about that. She'd grown fonder of Hugh than she had realized; something inside her didn't want him to be the one the sheriff was looking for, and, she felt more guilty, something inside her didn't want to see him caught even if he did have something to do with that body in her wall. She couldn't bring herself to believe that the Hugh Coles she had come to know would have done anything like that except in self-defense.

Hugh had gotten electricity to some parts of the castle before he had disappeared. Jake Monroe had continued working on the castle, and the basic rooms Ally had wanted fixed up to live in during the bulk of the restoration had been finished the previous week, and Ally had been in residence there for three days. It wouldn't be long before Jake's crew would need another electrician, though. And the one Jake had brought in for Ally to meet was off on another extensive job in Lexington.

Even though Ally was quite peeved at Hugh for leaving her in the lurch, she also missed having him around the castle. He'd always been quick with a witticism or an appropriate comment on national or local events, and Ally had taken to eating a picnic lunch with him under the trees in the yard. Jake often took her to dinner, and quite often to expensive country restaurants. And when he did, he treated her like a princess. But she felt more comfortable and found she enjoyed the conversation better with Hugh in those days before he drove off the job. She probably should have known, she thought, that he was a lot better educated than the degree he'd produced for her indicated. He could have held his own in conversations with her worldly wise colleagues in the Foreign Service. He and she shared much the same ground in their opinions on national and world events, while Jake would teasingly mock her liberal leanings. She found she avoided topics in talking with Jake that she hadn't in her conversations with Hugh.

Of course Hugh was too young for her, and although she was about the same number of years younger than Jake, that age difference just didn't seem to matter much.

The negotiations had gone well in Luray. The story of the castle restoration, riding on the discovery of the body in the wall, had traveled fairly widely already—as had the side tale that Ally had survived a terrorist bombing in Jordan before returning to Virginia—and the lumber supplier was anxious to have his company's name attached to her effort. He thus gave her a good cut in costs in exchange for her permission to use the castle connection in his advertising and with any newspapers he could get to run the story in the valley.

She was celebrating her good fortune by treating herself to lunch at the artsy Artisans Grill on the main downtown street of Luray. She'd finished with a sampler salad and was perusing the dessert list when she was stunned to hear a familiar voice saying her name.

"Well, hello there, Ally. What's brought you to Luray?"

It took Ally a moment to lift the jaw that had dropped nearly to the table top at seeing Hugh Coles standing there beside her table, cool as he could be, wearing a natural smile, and giving no indication that he was hiding from anyone.

"Hugh. What are you doing here? Don't you know you're wanted over in Washington."

"Yeah, I heard. May I sit?" He laughed at her reaction to that. "We're in the middle of a crowded restaurant. Do you think I'm going to be a mad killer in here?"

"No, I guess not," Ally answered, with a somewhat nervous laugh, though. "You left me high and dry, you know."

"Yes. Sorry about that. I was going to come across the mountain this afternoon and talk to you about that. And I was going to stop at Sheriff Shiflet's office first. I've been tied up. Still, I should have called. Sort of steeped in high drama for a while, though."

"I guess being wanted for questioning for murder can do that to a man," Ally countered.

It was Hugh's turn to give a nervous little laugh at that. He was sitting at the table now, though not really sitting at the table. He'd reversed a bentwood chair and was straddling it backwards. This, with the baseball cap turned backwards, made him look boyish and a bit like he was going to launch from the table at any minute and up the split staircase at the back of the restaurant.

Ally tried to calm down, because she really didn't want him to leave until she got some semblance of an explanation from him on why he had left—and, possibly more important, why he had been there in the first place if he had a doctorate in engineering.

"So what kept you from contacting either me or the sheriff earlier? And, more important, why did you skip out on me?

And, be advised, those are just my preliminary questions if you stay around here long enough to hear the others."

"How about what to have for dessert first. My treat. I did tell one of the EMTs to tell you I had to go. He didn't pass the word on?"

"No, no one told me you checked out that day."

"Sorry, then. Really my bad for not contacting you before now. Will buying you two desserts make up for that? They serve them good here."

"In that case, the blueberry cobbler and a cup of coffee." She couldn't help but give a little laugh at how neatly he had segued into that.

"Same for me, Donna," he said to the waitress who had miraculously appeared on cue. He turned back toward Ally and gave her a little grin.

"Anyone ever tell you you had a nice laugh—and a husky voice. Just like that actress, you know . . ."

Ally didn't save him. She wanted to know if he'd come up with what so many others did—and then he did.

". . . Kathleen Turner. That's it. That sexy husky voice. Not that I'm saying anything by that. But you look quite a bit like her too." He was blushing.

Ally felt like she was blushing too—at the pleasure of the comparison that others had also made in the past. But she jerked herself back into the present. "Donna? You called the waitress by name. You know her?"

"Yes. Everyone knows Donna in this town. This is my town. I know the sheriff has been looking for me here, but I'm from Luray and everyone knew I had something important to attend to here that couldn't be put off. Luray folks watch out for their own. I was born and raised here."

"Before you went off to Georgia Tech?"

"Yes, before that."

"And before you got a doctorate from Georgia Tech in electrical engineering but decided that you'd use that to string wires in people's houses?"

"Ah, you know about that."

"Yes, the sheriff was quite knowledgeable about your past."

"Ah. Well, then, perhaps I should first answer the question why I left the castle without giving you proper notice that day."

"That would be a good place to start, yes."

"It ties in with some of the rest. One aspect of the answer is just what you said. Sheriff Shiflet is quite knowledgeable about my college boy past. I sowed a lot of my oats in his neighborhood because my family wouldn't stand for me to do it over on this side of the mountain. Guess you noticed that Jake Monroe and I don't get along very well."

"Yes, I have." Ally answered. What she didn't say was that she fancied that the two were in some sort of struggle for her attention. She did think that was a factor, and it was a struggle that she couldn't help but take as flattering as both were good looking intelligent men.

"A lot of it is that his younger half-brother, Craig, ran with the gang I was running with. I suppose Jake thinks I was misleading his younger brother, but the truth is that Craig was the one who came up with most of the hell-raising ideas. I think Jake has had it in for me ever since then. Boys will be boys in rural Virginia, though, and I guess I was a bad boy with the best of them. Not much I can do about that now. Best I can say is that I straightened out and went to Georgia Tech and got those degrees. I earned those with hard work, by the way."

"The quality of your work on the castle shows it. But that's only an aspect to the answer."

"Yes. You probably noticed I wasn't there that morning when you arrived. I had been called home, over here in Luray. Because my father was dying. I only came back to the castle to get my Airstream and to tell you I had to be gone for a while— probably not more than a couple of weeks based on the prognosis my dad had been given. Then I got over there and saw the ambulance and all the cop cars—and Sheriff Shiflet, who I didn't ever want to see face to face again, and I just gave a message to an EMT to pass to you when you had settled down from the shock you got, and then I split. I could see you sitting on the back of the ambulance, and one of the cops I knew told me what they'd found inside the castle. It didn't have anything to do with me, so I split. And I'm sorry about not calling you after that, but it got pretty dicey with my dad. He didn't go into that good night easily. He always was a cantankerous soul. Put my mother in the grave I think because of his difficulty. He's what I was modeling on when I got into all that trouble over on this side of the Blue Ridge. Anyway. No one else would come within ten feet of him in the end, so I was stuck at his bedside. Not at home. In a nursing home, which is probably why Shiflet never found me."

"And how is he—your father?"

"He's dead now. He died yesterday. That's why I was going to come over the mountain today."

"I'm sorry to hear that."

"As I said, he was a cantankerous soul. And now he's free. So are the rest of us. End of story, I think. Other than I'll have to come back for the cremation in a couple of days. I'll need time for that—if, of course, you still need and want me back on the job."

Hugh was looking down at the table top, unable to look Ally in the eye. Her heart went out to him, and not just because of the painful story he had just related to her. The effect of his boyish good looks and being exposed to his vulnerable side was stirring something inside Ally, something she hadn't felt since Chad's reaction of awe when she'd first given herself to him. She leaned over and put a hand gently on his arm. He turned his face up at her then, with a look of surprise and utter gratitude. Their eyes locked for only a second, but Ally felt the electricity in the brief moment, and she thought that Hugh did as well.

They were sitting in the middle of a restaurant during the lunch hour. This was neither the time nor place. She didn't know if she really wanted there to be a time a place at all. But this was not it. She looked away.

"I think it might be more complicated than that," she said. "Your coming back on the job at the castle."

"How so? You don't want me around for other reasons? Had it become too obvious that I liked talking with you, being with you?"

"Oh, no, nothing like that." She was really blushing now, completely caught off guard. "I hadn't been thinking that at all. I don't know how anyone would get that idea. I'm several years older than you for starters."

"Not all that much older," Hugh muttered. "What, four or five years? That doesn't mean anything."

It was only then that Ally realized her hand was still lightly placed on his arm. She pulled it away with a guilty twinge and turned her head from him. When she looked back at him, he looked a little confused—like he knew something had just happened, but he wasn't sure what. And more than that, he wasn't sure what had broken the spell.

"It might be difficult for you to come back to work," she said, "because Sheriff Shiflet is looking at you as a murder suspect—for that body found in my wall."

"A suspect in that murder? I didn't know that. I just thought he wanted a statement from me on what I knew about whatever."

Ally gave him a hard look. "I swear I didn't know that, Ally. I didn't think that that had anything to do with me. All I thought was that I had to be off the job and taking care of my dad for a spell . . . honest." The last was said, haltingly, because Ally hadn't changed her expression.

"The sheriff thinks you were working at the castle about the time they estimate the body was put in the wall."

"How did he get that idea? I've never worked at the castle before."

"Jake Monroe told him he thought you had."

"Well, Jake Monroe is . . . wrong about that."

The way Hugh had hesitated made Ally think that he really wanted to say that Jake was intentionally lying about that. For what reason? To clear the way to her for Jake? Did Jake see Hugh as a threat in that way? Perhaps she'd been so numb to the world that she hadn't seen this dynamic develop on her construction crew.

"I guess Sheriff Shiflet needs to hear that directly from you, then," she said to Hugh, not wanting to think about anything more complicated in her life than that. "And you need to convince him, or he isn't going to stop hassling you."

"OK, I swear I'll go directly from here over to Washington and talk to him. If I clear that up, do I still have a job at the castle?"

"I haven't been able to find a replacement yet. So, you talk to the sheriff and we'll see what he does before I make a commitment on that."

"Do they know who the body is—was—whatever?"

"Not yet, but I trust we'll have an ID sometime soon. The sheriff thought it would be a couple of weeks, and it's almost that now. If they know anything, they aren't releasing it. And, there are more questions. Like why the mysterious appearance looking for an electrician's job with a professor's background?"

"You talked to me about why you were back in Virginia and why you were restoring the castle. And I didn't tell you anything about the place I was at, did I?"

"No you didn't. I felt that was a bit one-sided even then. There aren't too many people I can talk to about my Chad—even if my mother wasn't fading away mentally she would not have wanted to hear about Chad—or any other man. But you were a good listener and I opened up to you."

"And all that time you were opening up to me, I wanted to be opening up to you too. But I just couldn't. It was too soon and too painful."

They sat in silence for a few moments.

"You aren't going to press me on it, are you?" he asked.

"If you want me to know, you'll tell me. If you aren't comfortable telling me, it will be no different than before. It was good for me to talk about it. But it was pretty one-sided, you know."

"I know. I know it would have been better if I'd talked too. Thanks for not pressing, but it's really pretty simple."

Silence again, as she waited him out.

"I wasn't alone at Georgia Tech. I was married. Her name was Ann. She was working on a doctorate too—in poetry. Imagine that, a poet trying to be married to an electrical engineer. You can just imagine the deep conversations we could have in sharing our work." He gave a dry laugh. His face was contorted in an inner pain.

"And she left you?" Ally asked quietly. She couldn't help it. This long pauses were getting to be too painful for her.

"In a way, yes. We were going to have a baby." Another pause. "I lost them both."

"Ah."

"So I was escaping. I came home to Luray, although I didn't really want to be in Luray, even though folks here were bending over themselves to be supportive. They knew about my wife and baby—it's probably a good bit why they haven't been telling Sheriff Shiflet where he could find me. Still, I didn't want to be around my dad any more than anyone else did—and especially not under the circumstances in which I'd come home. I heard about someone working up at the castle. So, I took Dad's old Airstream and I came up there. And you know the rest."

"Yes, now I know the rest."

"And I was just about to tell you all that when my dad decided to die—and to take his time doing it—and you decided to take that wall down yourself. I never could fault my dad on his timing being malicious."

They sat there in silence, each staring at the congealed cobbler and the cold coffee that neither had touched.

"We can't eat those now," he said.

"No," she said.

"Shall I have them rustle up another round?"

"No, I think not. I don't have the appetite for cobbler any more today. And my guess is that you don't either."

"No, I guess not. But I promised you a dessert."

"You can get me one someday when we've worked hard up at the castle and need a nice break."

"Thanks," he said. His voice sounded a bit choked up, knowing by what she'd said that he was welcome back on the job. If he'd been looking at Ally closely, he probably could have told that he was welcome to much more than that.

* * * *

Hugh Coles arrived at the castle that afternoon about two hours after Ally had done so. She had meant to pick her mother up at Lois's and take her up to the castle for a half hour or so for the first time that day. But the meeting with Hugh had pushed her off her stride and she decided she'd do that another day. When Ally got to Banffy, she found Jake and his crew busy there. They were working on putting the flooring back in between the first story and the second in the central section, which was a major job. After this was done, one crew could work on refinishing the first floor, and another crew could be brought in to work on the walls and a roof over the second story. The intricate woodwork and plastering would have to wait until that section of the castle was back under roof. The work was going very fast; the interest in the project had attracted workers, and Ally had the money to pay them.

They were really making progress now Ally could see as she drove up to the building. And they really needed an electrician working full time as well. There was electricity to the building, but not nearly enough plug-ins for the number of tasks that now needed to be going on at once.

She went to her rooms and changed and came out, hard hat and all, and walked around, doing her contractor "thing," and making sure all of the men and women were doing what they were supposed to be doing. Since the escapade where she took the sledgehammer to the partition wall in the ballroom, Jake had backed off on trying to change her mind about anything that she said she wanted done. He no longer was questioning if that was the way she wanted it. Now it was a discussion on how they were going to get done what she wanted done. All of the construction workers were giving her added respect as well.

The rumble of the Airstream being pulled back up the road through the grape vine stands was enough to bring all of the workers to a door or window to check it out. Jake came too, and Ally didn't miss the big frown that swept across his face when he realized that Hugh was coming back. Ally hadn't bothered to tell Jake this ahead of time.

Perhaps she should have, she now thought. Jake looked like he didn't like this development at all.

As Hugh parked the Airstream right where it had been before, Ally went out to meet him.

"You weren't as long as I expected," she said.

"There wasn't much the sheriff could do. I gave him telephone numbers he could call in Luray to verify where I'd gone—and why. Some of the leading citizens there are ready to back me up, so he didn't give me a lot of grief about that. And as far as me ever having worked at the castle before, he didn't have any proof I had—at least yet, he said. So, as long as he knew I was going to be up here, he said, I could be here instead of in his jail. He admitted he didn't have enough to hold me on any charge and said things might be different when the body was identified. He said something about having learned that some of the guys I ran with up here during my college summers weren't accounted for. That doesn't surprise me a bit, though. A lot of them were drifters."

"I'm glad he let you come on up here," Ally said. "There's plenty of work needing to be done."

Hugh looked a bit amused. "That's what I told the sheriff, and he became almost cooperative after that. I got the impression that he's just a bit scared of you. What do you have on him?"

Ally fought hard not to show Hugh that he'd hit a mark he was only joking about.

"I think he's beginning to see the tourist industry possibilities of a completed castle," she said. It was a bit weak for a rejoinder, but Hugh obviously wasn't serious and didn't expect a logical response.

They were both turned so that they could see the façade of the castle, and Jake was still standing there in the entry door, glaring out in their direction.

"Guess I should go check in with Jake," Hugh said. "I think I've got a bone to pick with him."

As he turned to go, Ally reached out and put a hand on his arm. He looked down at her hand and then back up into her eyes. His face had the same expression on it that he'd had when she'd touched him in the Luray café.

"Ally," he said in a strangled voice.

"Not now, Hugh. People are watching. Jake is watching."

"But surely sometime."

"Yes . . . I think . . . sometime. Now go on and talk to Jake. But try not to get too belligerent about it," Ally said. "That's why I stopped you. I don't want any fighting now. I need both of you working together on this project."

"Yes, ma'am, boss lady," Hugh said, not being able to keep a grin from stealing across his face.

Ally watched him stride across the lawn and driving circle to where he stood facing Jake from below the entry. They both were standing rigid, with clinched fists, obviously talking to each other in tense tones. It didn't last very long, though. Both turned their faces toward Ally, and she knew that one or both of them were saying exactly what she'd told Hugh—that she expected them to work together without a lot of display of animosity. There was only one construction foreman here. It was Ally. If she wanted Hugh working here, that was her call. But if she wanted Hugh to keep out of Jake's way as much as possible, that was her call as well.

After she could see that World War III wasn't happening, she walked around the side of the building, checking the walls for cracks. When she got to the back of the building, her eye picked up movement from the direction of the overgrown fire trail that she'd seen Jake's red truck go up the day of her first return to Banffy. The movement materialized as a hiker, coming down the trail. He stopped as soon as he realized that there was a castle rising again from the plateau and gawked for a moment. Seeing Ally, he walked to her, picking his way through the overgrown ornamental garden. Ally stood there and waited for him to approach. She hadn't seen a hiker coming down here from the

Appalachian trail since she'd returned to Virginia. But she'd seen them occasionally when she was in her teens and living here. She assumed that this was where the mountain man, Hank Morris, who had harassed her mother had come from that summer before Ally went to college.

She steeled herself. The young man looked harmless enough, but the memory of her mother's trouble with a man coming from that direction put her on edge. He was dark skinned and was wearing first-class hiking gear, with a backpack, and looked pretty clean cut to Ally. He didn't look like a country boy.

"Hello," he hailed her when he was some thirty feet away.

"Hello, yourself," she called back. "Are you lost? The trail's at the top, behind you."

"No, I'm not lost. My name's Tom Black," he said as he drew closer. "I won't play games here. I'm a features reporter with the *Washington Post.* I've been talking with one of your contractors, Jake Monroe. He said there were several good stories here. I saw one of them as soon as I came off that trail. This looks like a real castle. Is it?"

"It was once. And it will be again, Mr. . . . Black, did you say? And Jake told you there was a good story here? Why are you coming from the mountain?" She was so confused by that, she wasn't thinking of the more obvious question of what she felt about the press being here.

"Mr. Monroe said he didn't know if the police would still be here when I could arrange to come—he said I might be stopped at the bottom of the hill."

"But still you thought you'd be welcome up here?"

"Jake seemed pretty sure you wouldn't bite me."

They shared a little chuckle over that. He continued. "There are great stories here. I wouldn't be a nuisance, I promise. There's the mystery of the body you recovered from the wall. And you and your ordeal in the Middle East make a story in themselves—"

That quite evidently wasn't the right thing to say, and he looked like he'd swallow that last sentence if he could. But of course he couldn't.

"I have no interest in a story being published on my experiences in the Middle East. And I imagine the State Department wouldn't want that either. So, if that's—" Ally turned to leave him standing there alone.

"No, please, wait. We don't need to go into that if there's a problem. But the crime story, that's really free game one way or the other. I don't want to upset you, though. Because I see an even better story now."

"A better story?"

"The castle itself. The restoring of the castle. And that you are doing the contracting yourself. This is going to be a beautiful building, I know. You must want to share it with others. I see a series of articles following the restoration as you go along."

"I don't know . . ."

"Jake says you hope to sell the place after you restore it. The publicity would be great for doing that quickly at a really good price. There aren't many who will be able to afford something this spectacular and will want this location. You will reach them with a *Post* series."

"Well . . ." He was making good sense. But she was going to have something to say to Jake about this.

Sensing victory, Tom Black was already fishing around in his backpack and pulling a notebook computer out.

* * * *

Ally was sitting in a dressing gown at her mother's dressing table, in a pool of light from a bare bulb hanging from a cord overhead. She was brushing her hair and examining for perhaps the thousandth time the left side of her face, trying to decide whether anyone could tell that it had been partially reconstructed. And how did it compare to how she'd looked before? She wasn't sure she even remembered how her face had looked before. And how would it look ten years from now? Would there be anyone who cared ten years from now? How old would Hugh be when she was forty-five?

"It's perfection."

She didn't flinch. She had sensed that she wasn't alone in the shadows of the castle. When she'd first been aware of it, she had wondered what she wanted to do, how she would react to the presence. But she had already decided. She looked toward the doorway to the suite of rooms she had made out of her mother's last stand in the castle. He was standing in the doorway, arms crossed, just in sleeping shorts, leaning against the door frame.

"I thought I heard something in the night in the central section. I came to check it out."

"Yes, thanks," she said. She wondered whether Hugh understood what she was saying yes to.

"I think if anything was there I must have scared it off."

"Yes."

"I meant to tell you something the other day—in the café in Luray, when we were talking about that day I left without telling you personally I was going."

Ally said nothing. She sat there, hairbrush suspended in air, and looking at Hugh in the shadow of the doorway in the reflection of the mirror.

"I was being pulled two ways that day. Hard. My dad was dying and even though we'd never gotten along, I think a son owes it to his dad to be there at the end—even if no one else is."

Another brief pause. Ally didn't move. She didn't even feel like she could take the next breath.

"I saw you there, sitting on the end of the ambulance, the blanket held tightly around your shoulders, and trembling something awful. There was nothing more I wanted to do just then than come and sit beside you and hold you and tell you everything was going to be all right. But I knew that if I came near you—even to say why I had to go—I wouldn't have gone. And, well, you are strong and alive and, with you, I could hope that there would be a future. But with my dad . . ."

He couldn't finish the sentence and Ally gave him no help.

Hugh cleared his throat and then spoke again in a low voice. "Well, I just needed to say that, and if there's nothing, I think I will . . ."

"Yes," she said, standing and turning and reaching for the tied ribbon holding her dressing gown closed.

Chapter Seven: The Great Leap

"I don't think it would be a good day for you to take her up to the castle—or even to come down here to see her, Ally."

"I'm sorry to hear that," Ally told Angela Harris over the telephone. "I thought she was becoming increasingly more aware and that it was time to reintroduce her to the castle."

"That may be the problem."

"Come again?"

"It's not that it's a bad day today because she is hazy; it's not a good day because she's more lucid than normal and has remembered the contract we had. I've continued to tell her that I just can't help her depart this world. But there's a new wrinkle now. She's saying that if I won't do it, then you have to do it. If you do come down to see her in the next few hours, you'd better be armed to deal with that."

"Thanks for the heads up. Perhaps I'll pass on a visit this morning, and we'll see if that's a fleeting notion or not. I couldn't do that anymore than you could."

"At least when it's not a physical issue—that she's not in perpetual pain—and as long as there might be a medical breakthrough to arrest this." Angela answered.

Ally tensed up. She wasn't sure herself if she could help her mother die even barring those circumstances. But Miranda and Angela had been so close for so long that Ally had to take Angela's views seriously.

She felt a sigh of relief travel through her when she disconnected the phone, but then felt guilty about it. She wasn't doing as much as either Lois or Angela for Miranda. She knew that was best for her mother, but she still felt guilty. It wasn't helping that she was growing ever closer to Hugh. She knew her mother wouldn't approve of Hugh—or, indeed, any man. But she still felt guilty that she was giving Hugh attention that she wasn't giving her own mother in her waning days. It didn't help that the model that Hugh had provided was to concentrate on the parent who was in the process of passing, because relationships with others had more of a future. Of course the sudden death of Chad didn't fit into that model all that well.

Her increasing connection with Hugh was beginning to take its toll on the construction site, and this was why she was secretly relieved she didn't need to go down the mountain to Washington this morning as she had scheduled. Jake wasn't taking the presence of Hugh well at all, and Ally suspected that Hugh, much younger than Jake, was quietly egging the other man on. Jake's growing ire wasn't obstructing work yet, but everyone was tense and tiptoeing around, waiting for something to happen.

And it was all under the scrutiny of the *Washington Post.* Tom Black and his photographer weren't being nuisances. They were full of good humor and the artisans—and Ally herself— enjoyed being asked questions about what they were working on, what tools and techniques they were using, and what effect they were after and then seeing this translated to articles twice a week in the *Post.* His presence had actually sped the work along and, Ally thought, most likely kept quality standards up. It gave the workers an extra charge of pride in their work, and it attracted highly skilled carpenters and artisans to the project.

The real problem of the attention by the *Post* was the curious onlookers it brought with its newspaper coverage. They came alone, in pairs, by the busload—up the road through the vineyard or down the fire trail from the Appalachian trail, as Tom has initially done. They set up picnic lunches out on the lawn to watch and, more annoyingly, wandered close around the workers, asking sometimes hilariously dumb questions and more often giving unwanted advice. It was this latter activity that was becoming irritating and wasn't helping the tension caused by Jake and Hugh's dance, apparently of age-old male supremacy for the attentions of a woman.

Well, Ally had news for both of them. She wasn't some trophy for any man. She made her own choices. And, news for Hugh, she hadn't made a final decision in this instance either.

Her thoughts were smashed, though, by the other problem—the wandering tourists. She could hear the cursing of one of the workman now. Yes, it was a good thing she didn't have to go down to Washington this morning, she thought, as she rose from her desk with a sigh and went in search of a situation that needed to be diplomatically calmed down.

* * * *

The next two weeks were a whirlwind. Ally finally had to call in her chit with the sheriff and obtain help with the curiosity seekers showing up to look at the castle on the basis of the *Washington Post* series. All she had to do really, though, was to say, "The first time one of them gets hurt up here, especially if they wandered off in the forest above the house, the first question will be why was there no control over the property—I do have 'No Trespassing' signs out and they aren't doing a bit of good. And who knows what they might trip over up there in the woods."

Sheriff Shiflet promptly sent a deputy up to take those signs down from the front lawn of the castle and move them up to the verge of the forest at the back of the house. The deputy then put up a rope line along the drive in front instead, from which spectators could get a good view of the construction progress but could be herded back to if they tried to get mixed up with the work. Shiflet didn't mind devoting the manpower, he said, because the restaurateurs and antique dealers down in the village of Washington were delighted with the extra business. The out-of-town traffic also paid for the extra police attention in what was added to the sheriff's department budget from the speed traps Shiflet set up around town. Even the local children benefited, as they set up soft drink and cookie stands to serve the visitors. The owners of the Mountain Castle winery were ecstatic.

The central portion of the castle now was under roof, and skilled carpenters were crawling all over the two floors in the main section, pouring over the photographs and sketches previously existing of this structure and of the one in Transylvania it was modeled from, and working wonders. Master carpenters were showing up in droves. No one else in the region was putting such ornate woodwork as this in their buildings.

The project was obviously becoming very expensive, especially as the work started moving into the artistic embellishments. Both Jake and Hugh were making noises about the cost. Jake, who clearly wanted the project to continue, kept mentioning that, with the *Post* coverage, which Ally never let him forget he had instigated, and the uniqueness of what was happening here and the setting, banks would loan her restoration money if she needed it, and that she was sure to turn a profit when she sold the place to some billionaire, the extremely well heeled having the habit of flocking to the Virginia countryside anyway. She just had to wait it out. And Hugh mentioned almost daily that he had inherited money and he'd help float her. She just agreed with Jake and told Hugh that she appreciated his offer but had no intention of calling on his help. She was reticent to tell either of the men that she, herself, was a millionaire, thanks to her great-grandfather's strange turnabout in acknowledging his descendents and her mother's frugality. She just didn't want to have the added element of either man knowing she had money.

The workers were all toiling merrily away, pleased to be part of such a high-profile project—and to be able to list it on their résumés—at least it was this way for a week after the security rope was put up. While they were working, though, they were also buzzing about the mystery of the corpse in the wall. The word had gone out that the lab tests on the body were, at last, finished and the results had gone to the State police. An identification surely was about to be made.

Then on a Friday afternoon, the animosity that had been seething between Jake and Hugh came to a head.

Ally was on the second floor of the central wing, doing a video interview with Tom Black on the detailed plasterwork being applied to the ceiling of one of the front bedrooms, a video that would run on the *Post*'s website, when she heard the surge of crowd noise below and in front of the building such as one would hear at a boxing match. She—and Tom and his video photographer, as well—hurried to a window on the front and looked down into the forecourt. Jake and Hugh were rolling around on the ground and throwing punches, some of which were connecting with an alarming thud. They were fighting inside a ring of workman that had quickly gathered around them. Most of the construction workers had suspended their work and obviously were enjoying the fight. Only the women carpenters seemed to be more interested in carving than watching.

She called down for the two men to stop and for the others to disperse and get back to work, which, of course, they didn't even hear over the crowd noise. Turning and looking for something to help make her be heard, she picked up a strip of tin that was being used for the ceiling installation of a nearby bathroom. Then she turned to a workman who was enjoying the fight from one of the windows in the room; yelled for him to give her his hammer, which he did; and then went to the window and banged on the tin with the hammer until everyone, including Jake and Hugh, both already with bloody noses and swelling eyes, looked up at her in surprise. The crowd quieted down.

"That will be quite enough of that, gentleman. I would like to see both of you out by where you've parked your truck, Jake. Now, please, gentleman."

When she'd pulled the two men away from where the workers could hear the conversation, she turned and looked at Hugh. She had placed herself between the two men, who were still posturing their belligerence.

"I won't even ask who started it—and why," she said. "Both of you need to cool off. Hugh, I suggest you go to your trailer for a while. Jake, I'm going to have to ask you to take the rest of the day off. Please leave."

"With pleasure, your highness," Jake growled through clinched teeth. "Come on guys, let's go."

"Just you, Jake. The crew can keep working."

"Most of these are my men, Ally. If I go, they go. I said come on guys, I'm calling this job site closed down."

Ally felt pressure at her elbow and realized that the *Post* videographer was getting the whole scene on camera. Looking on the other side of her, she saw a grinning Tom Black. His expression immediately changed when he realized that Ally was looking at him. "Sorry, but this is great news drama," he said. And then when he was still met with a frown. "But you're amazing; it will be just as good news seeing how you work this out."

Ally never saw Jake on the construction site again. And some of his crew didn't return either. She could continue work only because most of the master craftsmen were direct hires and didn't work for Jake.

She took Tom Black's statement that it would be "good news seeing how" she'd work this out as encouragement and became quite businesslike in walking around and assessing where projects stood and who was left to work on them. She didn't want to show any indication that she was either throwing in the towel or panicking. She took the reporter and his photographer—as well as Hugh Coles—along with her for the next three days as she went to Luray and also as far as Harrisonburg and Front Royal to recruit a new set of construction workers for the project. In the end, many of the men and women who had been there under Jake's subcontract came back to work directly for her. Both the publicity and the pay were good, and, as it turned out, Jake didn't just leave the construction site, he disappeared altogether—and, it turned out, he seemed to have left with most of his company's funds.

Within days the restoration work was back in full swing, Tom Black said he had dynamite material for his *Post* series, and Lois and Angela were reporting that perhaps it would be good now for Miranda to visit the castle—that seeing it rising from the ashes as quickly as it was might be beneficial for her.

Ally wasn't so sure the timing was good the morning she came down to Lois's farm to pick her mother up. Miranda's awareness seemed to be drifting in and out. But she was placid enough, claimed to recognize Ally, and kept patting her daughter's arm and giving her affectionate smiles as they drove up through the winery and into the turning circle at the front of the castle, telling Ally rather nonsensically that everything would be all right, as if Ally were the patient. Ally kept looking furtively at her mother as soon as the castle came into view to see what effect seeing it had on Miranda. But if Miranda noticed anything special at all, she didn't react.

Ally had asked Hugh to stay in his trailer while her mother was there to avoid any chance of Miranda seeing him. And she made similar requests to the men among the construction workers, asking them to work somewhere else other than in the area extending from the grand foyer, past the ballroom, and to the quarters that had once been her mother's and that now had been restored for Ally's use.

"It's going to be lovely someday," Miranda murmured as she looked around the grand foyer. Ally couldn't tell from that if Miranda had any idea where she was. Ally stopped on purpose at the door leading into the ballroom, which was partially restored and had been returned to its original dimensions.

"This is the ballroom, Mother. Remember it?"

"It's big. I like smaller rooms."

"It had a partition dividing it at one time," Ally said. She was doing this on purpose. She remembered that the sheriff wanted to pin down when that partition had been put in and who had done the work.

"Of course, I remember," Miranda almost snapped with a "do you take me for a dummy" response. "I had it put in myself."

"Yes, you did, Mother. I'm glad you remember. Do you remember when it was put in and who you had do it?"

"Yes, of course I do," her mother shot back.

There silence reigned for several seconds.

"When was it and who did it, Mother?"

"Was what and who?" Miranda said, the ethereal tone of her voice telling Ally that she was at least momentarily in another world again. "I do believe I am thirsty. Could you ask Lois to bring in some Coke for us—with maybe a tad of whiskey in it?"

"Come on into your rooms, Mother," Ally said with a sigh. "We'll see what I have that I can give you."

Ally was stopped by one of the women woodworkers while they were moving to Ally's living quarters, and Miranda wandered around the construction site a bit, clucking at this and giving a low laugh at that, seemingly fully entertained by the reconstruction process.

Once in the suite of rooms Miranda herself had occupied for several years before she burned it out, Ally's mother forgot all about being thirsty. She moved from object to object, picking it up lovingly and examining it closely as if it was a long-lost friend. She was muttering about where and under what circumstance she had collected each piece. Ally had done what she could to arrange the room just as Miranda had had it. When Miranda came to the mantelpiece, she immediately put her hand on the silver cup with the "A.D." initials on it, but rather than picking it up, she muttered something in an ugly, growly voice and shoved the cup back toward the wall. Her hand then went immediately to a bisque statue of a French court couple in a romantic pose. Ally moved forward in half alarm that her mother would break the delicate figurine after the violent shove she'd given the silver cup. But Miranda held and examined the figurine as lovingly as she had the other objects she had picked up before finding the silver cup.

There was a masculine clearing of a throat at the open door to the central house, and Miranda almost dropped the bisque figurine in surprise. Ally was quickly there to hold Miranda's hand steady, though. Ally could feel her mother trembling—doubtlessly because of the intrusion of a man.

"Sorry, Ms. Templeton. But you did say to let you know when the paint you ordered had arrived—what they've been waiting for to use on what you say is the music room. They say you need to sign for it. I'm sorry, but—"

"That's quite all right, Eric, I'll come out and sign for it now."

She turned to her mother, suggested that she might want to sit and rest for a few minutes while business was attended to, and, once Miranda was settled in a club chair, Ally went to the kitchenette and poured a Coke into a glass, tipped in just enough whiskey to be able to truthfully claim to her mother that she had done so, and, after giving this to her mother, left the room.

As soon as Ally left the room, Miranda gave a sly little smile and rose from the club chair. She reached into the pocket of her dress and pulled out the cigarette pack with three cigarettes still in it that she had snatched off a stack of boards in the ballroom while Ally was talking with the woman woodworker. Miranda started gliding around the room, looking for matches.

There were a few other questions to address while Ally was out in the main section, but it couldn't have been more than fifteen minutes before she returned to her rooms.

No Miranda.

Ally looked everywhere in the suite of rooms without seeing her mother. She couldn't have gone farther into the maze

152

of what once was a servants' wing, because Ally had that locked off and the key placed someplace Miranda could not have quickly found it. She was about to leave the suite and start searching for Miranda in the formal areas of the castle when her eyes went to the staircase in the tower leading up four flights.

"Oh, no," Ally exclaimed as she raced for the stairs. She quickly checked each level of the tower on her way up to the battlements at the top of the tower. As she feared, when she got to the fourth level, she could see the hatch open to the top of the tower's open-air battlements. She struggled up the ladder and leaped out onto the stone-floored top of the tower.

She heard the gasps and hubbub coming up from the ground and rushed to the stone balustrade and looked down four flights to the ground. A shocked and murmuring group of workmen had gathered in a circle around the spread-eagled body of her mother, her arms and legs at impossible angles. Miranda was lying on the ground on her back, staring up at the top of the tower, a peaceful smile on her face.

Chapter Eight: Daddy Mine

"It wasn't anyone's fault, Ally," Angela said. "She wanted to go and we all know how strong her will was. If we wouldn't do it for her, she was determined to do it herself. I should have known, though."

"What do you mean?" Ally asked. They were sitting in the living room of Shadow Hill, Angela Harris's Washington home. They had just been to the cremation ceremony. Ally would be putting Miranda's ashes in the base of a fountain that would go in the ornamental garden at Banffy when the castle restoration was complete. There was no reason new owners need even know they were there. But Ally knew her mother would be pleased that no one could deny her eternal possession of the castle.

"The day before you took Miranda up to the castle, she was lucid enough to bring up the topic of our contract again. She told me that she knew and accepted that I couldn't do that for her—that our bond was too strong. She let me off the hook. I told her that her bond was just as strong with you and that you hadn't agreed to any such contract, and she said she knew and accepted that. I should have known then that she was taking the responsibility back on her own shoulders. I assumed, with relief, that it meant she was giving up the idea of ending her life. I was wrong. I should have known that this would be Miranda's way."

They sat in silence for a few minutes before Angela sighed and said, "I asked you to stop by today because I have something for you. Your mother had me keep a strongbox for her. She said it was just a lot of papers, but they'd be ones you needed when she was gone."

"You have Mother's papers? They didn't burn in any of the fires?"

"No they didn't burn. I had to laugh when she asked me to keep them. She said she was sure she'd burn the castle down someday because of her smoking habit—that you kept saying she would—and that she couldn't stop smoking, so she'd best have the papers kept somewhere else."

"Can I see the box now? It might contain something the sheriff wanted me to discover from her that would help with the case of that body in the wall in the ballroom."

Angela went upstairs and retrieved the box and Ally sifted through the papers inside it with trembling hands. Sure enough she came up with the paperwork on the partition wall that Miranda had put in the ballroom.

"I need to make a phone call," she said, almost beside herself with excitement and concern.

"Yes, that figures," Sheriff Shiflet said when she told him what she'd found. "The police ID just came in on the body in the wall. I was going to contact you as soon as you'd had a chance to have the memorial service for your mother. The body was that of Craig Monroe, Jake's brother and partner. He didn't just run away with the money four years ago. He didn't run away at all. He was murdered and walled up in the castle."

"And we know now that the Monroes are the ones who were putting in that wall—so it was Jake lying about that. So—"

"So Jake is probably our murderer. Those two were from two different mothers and they were always at each other's throats. I'm not a bit surprised that Craig is dead and Jake is gone. He got the money then and he's taken off with the money now too. He isn't just pouting somewhere; he's taken off."

"So you should—"

"Already in train, missy," the sheriff interjected. "And your mother is completely off the hook for taking her ornery ways toward men too far."

Ally told Angela that news when she and the sheriff had disconnected. She should have felt elated and relieved, but a nagging question remained. And it was a question she should have asked a long time ago. Angela readily agreed with that.

"My goodness, Ally. Why didn't you ask before? And I thought I told you. Dennis is in Prague. He couldn't have been the man in the wall at the castle. He's very much alive. I had to talk to him last week about some investments we still share."

"I was so afraid it was him—and that maybe mother did have something to do with . . . and that there was some secret about that between you two that would be devastating for me to bring up. I kept intending to ask. You did tell me he was in Prague, but I didn't think he really was there. I know wherever he was he'd be playing his violin in an orchestra. That's too big a part of his life. I had friends in the State Department scour the city of Prague for a Dennis Harris and they came up blank. So I thought he really wasn't there."

"Don't you remember that I told you he had changed his name when he came to the States?"

"Yes, but . . ."

"He changed it back when he went back to Prague. He's known as Antoine Donateley in Prague. And he does play for the Czech Philharmonic. You can find him readily enough—if you really want to. But you may not want to."

"Why is that, Angela?"

"I suppose it's time you knew. That was another thing your mother told me she wanted me to do when she spoke to me about dying the day before she plunged off that tower. She thought you should know who your father was—and even why she hasn't told you all of these years."

"I know what the speculation is," Ally said.

"The speculation is wrong. You think it's the conductor, August Donáti, don't you?"

Ally's expression revealed that she did.

"So did some other people, even though Donáti was sixty at the time. But he was in no way involved in your parentage. I've always told your mother that it was wrong to let that speculation float. But she didn't deny it. To protect me."

"To protect you?"

"Yes, Ally. You didn't figure out the significance of that record your mother had Lois give you, did you?"

"I assumed it was a clue that August Donáti really was my father. He conducted the music."

"You missed two key points then. First was the featured piece itself. Do you remember what that was?"

"'Elgar's Violin Concerto in B minor,' wasn't it?"

"Yes. But did you know that that concerto had another name? It was discussed in the notes on the record jacket. Did you read them?"

"No, I'm afraid not. I thought the message was less subtle than that."

"Well, when you go back to the castle, look at that record jacket again. The Elgar violin concerto is also known as 'Alice's Concerto.' It has been strongly suggested that he wrote the concerto for a woman named Alice Street-Wortley. 'Alice' is the important word here. Your mother named you Alice. It was such an old-fashioned name—and ultimately such a painful one for both her and me—that we quickly gave you the nickname 'Ally.' But your mother had originally used Alice as a sort of revenge and a statement that the circumstances would never be forgotten. She never gave you an idea where the name came from, did she? After she'd had you, though, and had fallen in love with having you, she couldn't live with that daily reminder of how she had gotten you."

"I asked about my name. No one in our family has that name. But she never would tell me. But why was it an act of revenge? Why is it significant?"

"Her first thought in using it was so that Dennis would never forget what he'd done—the shame of it."

"Dennis?"

"Yes, the second clue on the record jacket. There's a featured violin solo in the Elgar piece. Did you see from the record jacket who that featured solo artist was in that version?"

"Yes, I did see that. It was Dennis. Are you trying to tell me—?"

"Yes, that Dennis is your biological father. But it's more sordid than that. And here I still hesitate to say . . . but your mother told me that if you were told any part of it, that you should know it all."

"What? Do tell me."

It took Angela several moments to begin forming the words. "I'm sorry, child. You are a child of rape—not a rape of sexual desire but one of anger. And some would even say a justified anger."

"Dennis raped my mother, and I was the result of that?"

"Yes. But out of rage, not desire or lust. Desire was your mother's and my sin. It wasn't Dennis's. Surely you've seen through the years how close your mother and I were. We were as close as two people could get. We were lovers. Everyone could see that, I think, but Dennis. He was absorbed in himself and after our initial months of marriage, we more or less went our separate ways. He had taken up with a flutist. I knew of their affair, of course. But I didn't care. I already had Miranda. Dennis walked in on us one afternoon. He went into a rage that ended with him beating me and raping your mother—to punish me. Your mother hated men ever since then. And she refused not to have you. I have often thanked our lucky stars you were a girl and not a boy, though."

Ally sat quietly for a few minutes to let that sink in. She couldn't be surprised that Miranda and Angela had been lovers. It had been right before her eyes her entire life. "But the rumors that the conductor was my father?"

"That was partially Miranda's fault. She may have been the one to drop the initials 'A.D.' to torment Dennis with the danger that his deed would be uncovered. We couldn't really publicly accuse him of the act, because he could counter by revealing our affair. And in those days, our affair would have been more of a scandal then his moment of rage. His affair would be written off as men just being men and a man whose anger could be justified by having been cuckolded. My affair with your mother would have been seen as abhorrent.

"I don't even know if she was thinking that the conductor had those initials when she used them as a tease when asked. She probably was only thinking of Dennis's real name. His original name and the one he has gone back to, Antoine Donateley."

"The initials. Those were the initials on the cup on the mantel in mother's room—the one that gave her such a bitter reaction on the day she died when she saw it."

"Ah, yes. That was another one of your mother's angry responses at the time to what Dennis had done to her. Dennis had inherited some silver—very old silver pieces—that had come down through his family in Eastern Europe. It was a family tradition that all of the men have the same initials. And they put those initials on their silver pieces. That cup on your mother's mantle was one of a set. I have the other seven still, here in the dining room."

"I know," Ally said in a whisper. "I've seen them."

"In a fit of pique your mother took one of the cups and had it engraved on the other side."

"The inscription 'Forgotten Never.'" Ally whispered.

"Yes, that, precisely. So you've seen that. It was meant to have a double meaning. Only the three of use—Miranda, Dennis, and I—would know that it symbolized a shame that was never forgotten rather than a love. She kept it out on her mantelpiece so that Dennis would see it whenever he came to where she was living. Very soon, though, he just stopped coming to where she lived."

"So, when my mother came here to live . . ."

". . . Dennis had to leave, to move back to Prague. He's not an evil man, Ally. He just has a volatile temper and he's also a very self-centered man. In my observation, most highly talented musicians, whether they are men or women, are the same. But it was an act of anger that was in part, at least, justified and understandable.

"Miranda and I had been treating him shabbily—and we continued to treat him shabbily through the decades since then. We never broke our bond. Instead we broke his spirit. I had no idea, but obviously he loved me—or wanted to possess me—more than I understood when I went looking for love with your mother. At least that was what he told me when he later tried to justify his horrific action. We broke him, Miranda and I. But I can't say, even after all of these years, that I care. I'm the one who encouraged your mother to move here—to buy and live in Banffy. Dennis of course opposed that strongly and said he would have to leave me—that he'd go back to Prague alone—if Miranda came here. I rejoiced in that. I always chose your mother over Dennis. My greatest fear now is that he will want to come back."

The two drifted off into silence again, broken only when a clock on Angela's mantle chimed the hour.

"So, there you have it. You know all now—including having an inkling of why your mother was so bitter toward men in general. I never could be, even when I was willing to give my all to her. But then I never had happen to me what happened to her. It did not cloud her love for you, though, I must assure you of that. You were her whole world. I even came to be a bit jealous of you. I hope that, even knowing the full story, you will not suffer the bitterness toward men that she did. It was probably a deeper tragedy of her stubborn strain than not being able to give up the smoking."

"Thank you, no, Angela. It will not put me off men."

Angela gave her a sharp look, and then a twinkle entered her eye. "Perhaps there's one man in particular who doesn't put you off?"

"I think there very likely is."

"And he's nearby?"

"Just up the mountain."

"Then I think we are well finished here. Why don't you go to him?"

"I think that perhaps I shall."

~

Olivia Stowe

Olivia Stowe is a published author under different names and in other dimensions of fiction and nonfiction and lives quietly in a university town with an indulgent spouse.

Olivia's books are all available in both print and e-book from Cyberworld Publishing and at all good on-line distributors.

Olivia Stowe
at
Cyberworld Publishing

Mystery Romance
Restoring the Castle

The Charlotte Diamond mystery series
By The Howling
Retired with Prejudice
Coast to Coast
An Inconvenient Death
What's The Point?
White Orchid Found
Making Room at Christmas (Seasonal Special)

The Savannah Series
Chatham Square
Savannah Time

Olivia's Inspirational Christmas collections
Christmas Seconds (2011)
Spirit of Christmas (2010)